"A Toast To Knowing What You Want, And Getting It."

"A toast," Becca said.

Cam looked at her like she was the very thing he wanted. That made her feel warm all over and she knew no matter how hard she tried to keep this tame, it wasn't going to work. She wanted Cam. He was everything she liked in a man. She remembered the way they'd fit together when they'd made love, so perfectly, and she wanted him again.

"I have a confession to make," Cam said.

"And that is?" she asked.

"I'm going to kiss you before you get in the car tonight," he said.

She shivered and everything feminine in her came to attention.

"I was planning to let you."

Dear Reader,

I hope you have been enjoying meeting all the Stern brothers! Cam is up last and to be honest he was a hard nut to crack. So of course I had to find a little something unexpected to throw his way. And Cam handled it as I expected he would—with the same determination that he faces everything.

Becca is the perfect foil for Cam. Where Cam relies on family and the bonds of community he's created for his support, Becca is a lone wolf. She doesn't know how to ask for outside help and pretty much expects to be left on her own no matter what happens in her life.

I hope you enjoy this story!

Happy reading,

Katherine

KATHERINE GARBERA

REUNITED... WITH CHILD

Harlequin

Desire

Recycling programs
for this product may
not exist in your area.

ISBN-13: 978-0-373-73092-6

REUNITED...WITH CHILD

Copyright © 2011 by Katherine Garbera

www.eHarlequin.com

Printed in U.S.A.

Recent Books by Katherine Garbera

Desire

KATHERINE GARBERA

is the *USA TODAY* bestselling author of more than forty books. She's always believed in happy endings and lives in Southern California with her husband, children and their pampered pet, Godiva. Visit Katherine on the web at www.katherinegarbera.com, or catch up with her on Facebook and Twitter.

This book is dedicated to my sweet husband, Rob,
for showing me that happy endings
happen all the time in the real world.

Acknowledgments

A special thank you to my editor, Charles,
for all his insightful editing on this book.

One

What had she been thinking when she'd accepted this invitation?

Becca Tuntenstall really didn't have time to go to a charity function in the middle of the workweek. But considering her former boss had invited her, she felt that it was just the second chance she needed. She'd walked away from everything and everyone in this world almost two years ago, and now she was ready to get back to it.

She checked her lipstick one more time in the ladies'-room mirror at the glitteringly decorated Manhattan Kiwi Klub. She'd designed this interior and really thought it captured the sparkle of the city with a sophistication that wasn't really found in society anymore.

She left the bathroom and walked into the ballroom. Her former boss, Russell Holloway, stood facing her. He smiled when he saw her and waved her over. She fixed a smile on her own face and headed his way like the confident, brash woman she'd been two years ago.

"Becca?"

She stopped in her tracks as she heard the one voice she'd thought she'd never hear again.

"Cam?" she said, not having to feign surprise at all.

She stared at him for what seemed like a frozen moment in time, and a million memories rushed through her mind. She remembered how hard it had been to just walk away from this man. "What are you doing here?"

"Russell invited me."

"Uh...okay. But don't you live in Miami?"

"I do. But I do travel from time to time," he said wryly.

She flushed, realizing she sounded like an idiot. "I'm sorry. You are just the last person I expected to see tonight."

"Or ever?" he asked.

"Definitely," she said. He looked good, damn him. Cam was tall, at least six foot five, with thick, dark brown hair and eyes that were so blue she couldn't look away from him. He had a strong, stubborn-looking jaw and a clean-shaven face. He wore his tux with an ease that most men simply couldn't carry off. He looked very comfortable and so devastatingly handsome that she had a hard time thinking straight. But then Cam Stern was the son of a socialite and a pro golfer. He'd been born with a silver spoon in his mouth and had only seen his wealth grow since he'd become an adult. In fact, she doubted there was anything that Cam couldn't buy. She knew that well enough from her experience with him.

"Well, I've got to go," she said, fully intending to walk away from him and never speak to him again.

"That's not going to work, Becca," he said.

"Why not? I believe your last words to me two years ago were that if I didn't want to be your mistress we had nothing left to discuss," she reminded him. She'd long gotten over her anger at the way he'd thrown her confession of love back in her face. Hell, no, she hadn't. She still wanted to see him writhe. She still wanted him to feel the intense pain she'd felt when he'd said those words to her.

"I owe you an apology," he said. "I have no excuse for being so cold. I was…your confession was unexpected and I wasn't in a position to make a decision to put a woman on par with my business."

"I know that," she said. "Despite how bitter that sounded just now, I really have moved on. Let's start over."

"Over?"

"Yes, pretend you are just running into me again and I'll be more polite," she said.

He started laughing. "I have missed you, Becca."

She shook her head. "Is there no one else who makes you laugh?"

"Not like you," he said.

She smiled at him, but she wasn't about to let herself

fall for his good looks and easy charm again. Cam had done a lot more than break her heart. He'd left her shattered, and she'd had to rebuild her entire life and who she thought she'd be. "That's too bad."

"Yes, it is. What have you been up to?" he asked.

"I started my own business," she said.

"I have to confess I knew that. Russell has been singing your praises to me for a while now."

"He has? I wonder why," she said.

"Because Cam has a project that could do with your touch," Russell said, coming up to them. Russell was a New Zealand millionaire who, like Cam, had been born with more money than Midas. At forty-one, he was two years older than Cam, and he lived the life of an international playboy, jetting from one cosmopolitan city to the next, managing his chain of Kiwi Klubs.

She never turned down work, and she wouldn't if Cam had a legitimate offer for her. She rarely saw her clients, and she could probably manage a few days of face-to-face time with Cam.

"What project?"

"I had hoped to discuss business at another time," Cam said.

"Nonsense. What else would you two have to discuss?" Russell said.

"What else?" Becca asked. Her short, red-hot affair with Cam had also been super-secret. They'd met in her hotel room each night and had white-hot sex. She'd thought it was a whirlwind romance, but it had turned out that the reason Cam had been keeping her secret was that he hadn't wanted more than sex from her.

"What else indeed," Cam said. "I'm not sure if you have heard any of the radio ads for Luna Azul's tenth anniversary celebration or not."

"I have heard them. Very good idea to advertise a Memorial Day weekend trip to Miami to be surrounded by celebs and balmy tropical weather."

"Thanks," he said. "That was my idea. Anyway, we have recently purchased a shopping mall that we are going to open as Luna Azul Mercado. And I'm looking for a designer for the project."

"And I thought of you," Russell said.

She opened her clutch purse, took out a business card and handed it to Cam. "I'd love to hear more about your project."

He took her card and glanced at it for a long moment before putting it in his pocket. "Business out of the way, perhaps we can enjoy the evening now. Can I get you a drink?" Cam asked.

"Gin and tonic," she said.

When he walked away, she was tempted to sneak out the back, but she'd paid a lot of money for her seat at this charity dinner with the intention of meeting a lot of Russell's friends and maybe securing more work for herself.

Becca doubted she would enjoy one second of tonight. There were few situations that she could think of that would be less fun than sitting next to two men from whom she'd kept important secrets. Russell didn't know that she and Cam had been lovers, and Cam didn't know that their affair had resulted in a child.

Cam had been prepared to see Becca again but he'd forgotten how he'd always reacted to her. One brief touch of her hand in his and his entire body had tingled.

Becca's heart-shaped face was pretty—not classically beautiful, but he couldn't take his eyes from her. Her nose was small and delicate, and her thick black hair was worn up with a few tendrils framing her face. Her mouth was full...seductive with that full lower lip, and he remembered the taste of her.

The scent of her had overwhelmed him, and he'd wanted to stand still and just breathe her in. He'd wanted to wrap his arms around her, plant his mouth on hers and say to hell with the last two years.

But he knew that wasn't going to be easy. He'd hurt her when he'd thrown her out of his life. He would never admit this to another person, but Becca had scared him and he'd had to walk away before he'd done something foolish—such as fall for her.

He got their drinks and walked back across the room. She stood talking to a well-dressed woman and looked up as he approached. She had a new life, he thought, watching her. She didn't need a former lover back in it. But he wasn't a man who gave up easily and there was only one thing he wanted...Becca Tuntenstall.

"Your drink," he said, handing it to her.

"Thank you. Cam, do you know Dani McNeil?"

"I don't believe I do," he said, shaking hands with the other woman.

Her hands weren't as soft as Becca's, and he didn't have any reaction to touching her. As though he needed proof that Becca was different—he'd already figured that part out.

"Dani works for Russell's foundation. She is the one who coordinated this tonight."

"Well done," Cam said. "I've attended a lot of parties and this one certainly ranks among the best."

Dani flushed. "Thank you. I've got to go check with the kitchen. I want to make sure everything is perfect." She walked away.

"I'm not sure I know many people at this function."

"I do," Cam said.

"Would you mind introducing me to some of them? I'm trying to grow my business."

"I'm not clear on what it is," he said.

"Tuntenstall Designers. I've designed interiors for hotels and nightclubs. I just finished work on a new hotel in Maui."

"Sounds like you don't need to grow too much," he said.

"There are always more hours in the day to fill," she said. "I'm afraid of running out of work."

"Has that happened?" he asked, wanting to know more about what made her tick.

"Not yet. But it could and I don't want that to happen."

He smiled. "You remind me a lot of me when I started the club."

"At least you had a trust fund to fall back on," she said.

He nodded. "That's true. But it didn't make the work any easier. And I was very conscious of the fact that if I failed I'd be putting my future and my brothers in jeopardy."

She quirked one side of her mouth. "I guess I didn't think of it that way."

"Why would you?" he asked. He was very aware that he and his brothers had cultivated an image of carefree playboys who'd never had to worry about anything.

"I hate it when people make assumptions about me," she said.

"We all do it," he said. "So who do you want to meet?"

"I really don't know. I heard that Tristan Sabina was here and he is a co-owner of Seconds nightclubs..."

"You want me to introduce you to the competition?" he asked. He was joking. Seconds was more competition for Russell's Kiwi Klubs than for Luna Azul. They had several branches in international hotspots instead of one dedicated location like Luna Azul. Someday Cam thought it might be nice to have another club, but he liked what they were doing in Miami. It would have to be just the right situation to tempt him to leave.

"Would you mind?" she asked.

"Not at all. In fact I know Tristan fairly well," he said, taking Becca's arm in his. He took a sip of his dirty martini and savored the salty taste.

"Do you need another drink?" he asked her.

"I'm good," she said. "Thanks for doing this."

"What?"

"Introducing me to Tristan," she said, drawing to a stop. "You don't have to."

"I know. I want to," he said. He'd let something slip away with Becca, and, to be honest, he regretted it. He hadn't been ready for her love two years ago, and he didn't know if he was now. But with his brothers settling down and Becca coming back into his life, he at least wanted to give it a chance.

He waved over Tristan, who was accompanied by his wife, Sheri. Cam made short work of the introductions.

"Becca is an interior designer," Cam said.

"*Enchanté, mademoiselle,*" Tristan said.

"It's a pleasure. I hope you don't mind but I asked Cam to introduce us so I could give you my card. I've done a lot of work for nightclubs and hotels."

"I don't mind at all," Tristan said. He took her card and pocketed it. "But I can't talk business tonight or Sheri will likely kill me." His French accent was very smooth and barely noticeable.

"I will," his wife said. "He's promised me a night out and I intend to hold him to it. We work together, so I hardly ever have a chance to just spend time with my husband that doesn't involve work or family."

"Then I'm sorry I brought it up."

"Not at all. So how did you start your own business? My boss can be a bear...I might want to do the same."

"You aren't quitting, Sheri, and leaving me alone at the office."

"Why not?" she asked her husband.

Tristan leaned down and whispered something in her ear that made her blush. Then she kissed him, and he put his arm around her. Cam wasn't sure what had been said, but he knew that it was intimate.

And he wanted that. He had been alone for a long time and had grown used to it, but there were times, especially now that his brothers were both engaged, that he wanted something more.

He glanced down at Becca and noticed that she was watching the married couple, as well. He'd ruined things with her once by not...by what? They'd had an affair. Affairs don't turn into love overnight. Cam Stern had always known he wasn't the kind of guy that women fell easily in love with. He was arrogant and difficult. He might know his way around a bedroom, and he knew he was the kind of lover who ensured his partner's pleasure, but a life together was about more than sex. He'd learned that the hard way.

The conversation at the dinner table was fun and lively, ranging from politics to economic trends to fashion. Becca wasn't sure she was going to fit in with the billionaires, scandalous heiresses and socialites, but she was managing to hold her own.

Seated around the table for eight were Russell and his supermodel date; Becca and Cam; then next to Cam, Geoff Devonshire—a member of the British royal family—and his new wife, Amelia Munroe-Devonshire; next to them were Russell's CFO, Marcus Willby, and his daughter Penny.

Despite the fact that she expected Cam to focus on

doing his own thing he didn't. He'd taken the seat right next to her at the table and introduced her to as many potential clients as he could. She wondered if he was trying to make up for breaking her heart all those years ago.

She was seated between Russell and Cam. The friendship between the two men was evident by the way they teased each other and joked around. She forgot about the fact that she intended to stay on her guard. To just get through this night as best she could. Until the topic turned to Luna Azul's Tenth Anniversary celebration over the upcoming Memorial Day weekend. "Did you invite Becca?" Russell asked.

"I didn't," Cam said, turning to Becca. "Would you like to come to the party as my guest?"

"You always have time to party," Amelia said with a smile.

Becca realized that she and Amelia lived in two totally different worlds. To a socialite, it was no big deal to jet down to a party in Miami. But to a working single mother, it was a huge affair. While she liked Amelia, Becca had a feeling she'd never be able to understand the way she lived.

"I own my own business so if I take too many days off, then I don't get paid," Becca said.

She wasn't going to let a table full of socialites pressure her into something she wasn't sure she wanted to do.

But Becca was curious. "Tell us more about the plans for the party."

Cam smiled. "Nate is working the celebrity angle

so we are going to have a room full of A-listers. Justin has smoothed over the tension we had in the local community and we will be combining the party with the groundbreaking for our new Mercado. That is the work I wanted to talk to you about," he said.

"We should probably discuss it later," she said, not wanting to talk business now.

"Definitely," he said.

"We can all give you some business advice, Becca," Russell said. "No sense letting you screw up the way I did early in my career."

"I can't imagine Russell making many mistakes," Amelia Munroe-Devonshire said. She was the guest speaker tonight. There was a time when she'd been more infamous than famous as the heiress to the Munroe hotel chain. But then she had married Geoff Devonshire last year and had been in the spotlight lately for her humanitarian work instead of her scandals.

"I have made more than my share, Amelia. I just managed to keep them out of the headlines."

"Touché! It's remarkably easier to stay out of the tabloids these days than it used to be. I can't believe it," she said.

Becca smiled at the heiress. She was funny and very fashionable but also down-to-earth—something Becca hadn't expected.

"That's because I keep a firm hand on the situation," Geoff said. Geoff was a minor member of the current royal family.

"I believe that," Cam added. "Both of you are of

course invited to the Tenth Anniversary Celebration in Miami."

"We are scheduled to be in Berne for a special award that Geoff's brother's mother is receiving," Amelia said.

"You must be proud of her," Becca said. Like most people she knew that Geoff and his two brothers had the same father but different mothers. The scandal that had rocked the world in the '70s when they'd been born had followed the men into adulthood and only last year when Malcolm Devonshire had died had it seemed to be put to rest.

"We are. Steven asked us to attend and we can't say no to family," Geoff said.

"No, you can't," Cam agreed. "That's why I now have a brother in New York while our business is based in Miami. Justin is up here helping his fiancée close up her apartment before she moves back to Miami."

Geoff laughed. "You do what you have to when it comes to family."

Family. It was something she seldom thought about except in relation to her eighteen-month-old son, Ty. Her father had left when she was two, and her mother had died of breast cancer when Becca was a junior in college. She'd been on her own for so long that it had never occurred to her that she'd taken something very precious from Ty until this moment.

Ty had uncles and a father who might want to know him. Might.

That was a big word to base her fears on. One thing

she knew for certain was that he'd never intended her to be the mother of his child.

She'd never intended it either.

The conversations turned to more private matters, and eventually Russell got up to introduce Amelia. Becca didn't know if she could sit at the table for another minute. She needed to get out of there.

She wanted to go back home to Garden City where there was comfort in the walls of the home she'd grown up in and in holding her sweet eighteen-month-old son.

As the lights went down and Amelia took the stage, Becca fumbled for her purse. It fell to the floor. Cam leaned in close, his big arm behind her.

"Are you okay?"

"Yes. I just need to step outside for a minute."

Cam reached down and picked up her handbag, handing it back to her. She pulled out her cell phone and saw that she'd missed a call from Jasper, her nanny. Finally some karma that might be good.

"I've got to go," she said, standing and weaving her way through the tables. She got to the lobby of the club and saw that it was crowded with patrons.

She made her way to a quiet alcove set off the main entrance. She sat down on a padded bench before calling Jasper back.

"It's Becca," she said as he answered the phone.

"Sorry to bother you," Jasper said. "Burt is sick so I had to take Ty to my house. I wanted to make sure you knew before you came home."

Burt was Jasper's twelve-year-old English bulldog.

"Not a problem. Thanks for letting me know. I might stop by and get Ty tonight."

"I figured you'd want to. I can even meet you at your house if you call when you are about fifteen minutes away."

"I will do that," she said, hanging up the phone.

She stood up and turned to leave the alcove but found that Cam was standing there.

"Everything okay?" he asked.

She nodded. "No emergencies."

"That's good. Amelia's done talking and they've opened up the dance floor."

"And?"

"I'd like to dance with you, Becca. We've never done that and it's been too long since I held you in my arms."

Two

Becca found herself pressed close to Cam on the dance floor a short while later. He smelled good, like expensive aftershave, and she had to really struggle to keep from resting her head on his chest. But she wanted to. It had been so long since she had anyone hold her, and she'd spent the last two years feeling very alone. She didn't need a man…she got on very well without one. But there was something about dancing with Cam to the slow bluesy song "Love Is a Losing Game" that Amy Winehouse had made popular a few years ago.…

"You're a good dancer," she said.

"My mother insisted on lessons. She might not have been too involved in her sons' lives, but she did make sure we were raised proper gentlemen."

"What does a proper gentleman do?"

"He knows how to talk to a woman, how to romance her."

"Romance? Is that what you are doing to me?" she asked. She hadn't gotten a chance to know the real Cam Stern when they'd had their affair, and though she'd thought she loved him, she knew that had been based on sex and quiet moments in the dark of night. She'd never danced with him or really even seen him outside of that hotel bedroom.

"I am," he said, pulling her close and spinning them around. Though the dance floor was crowded, she felt like they were the only two people in the room. His eyes were intense as he looked down at her. She felt as if they could bore all the way through to her soul and the secret she kept from him.

She should go. She should walk out of his arms and leave. She needed to remember that no matter how romantic the night felt, Cam wasn't the kind of man who was interested in settling down or starting a family. And she came with a ready-made one.

He kept his arms around her, and she told herself she was Cinderella and this was for only one night. Even Cindy had gotten one night with her Prince. She knew that Cam wasn't some white knight who could rescue her. She'd seen the chinks in his armor. But when he held her close like this, it was easy to forget about that all that. It was so easy for her to just pretend that for once she was going to have her cake and eat it, too.

"What are you thinking?" she asked, as she glanced up and found him staring at her.

"That you are the most beautiful woman in the room," he said.

She flushed and shook her head. "I'm not."

"In my eyes you are," he said. He leaned down, and the warmth of his breath brushed her cheek as he spoke directly into her ear. "You are the most exquisite woman I've ever seen. You have haunted my dreams."

"Then why did you wait so long to get back in touch with me?" she asked.

"I didn't think you'd be able to forgive me. And I wasn't sure if I had fantasized about you so much that I made you into someone you weren't. But none of that matters now."

But it did. He was talking to her as if nothing had happened except a bad breakup. But she knew there was so much more between them, and she had no idea how to tell him.

He wasn't the evil ogre she'd made him out to be. She'd known that even back then, but she had pride. Some said too much pride was a bad thing, but Becca didn't really know how to define "too much." She had only understood that Cam wasn't the kind of man who'd take the news of her pregnancy well.

She twisted and started to walk away from him.

He caught up with her and grabbed her arm as she reached the edge of the dance floor. "Where are you going?"

"I can't do this, Cam. I am trying to pretend this is all just a nice night out, but every time I look in your face I see the past. And I'm just not ready to deal with that tonight."

"I'm not asking you to," he said. "I think we should forget about what happened between us—"

"I can't. It's way too complicated to go into now, but trust me when I say I could never pretend we didn't meet."

"That's a good thing," he said.

She shook her head and pulled away from him. "No, it's not. There are things about me that you don't know."

"Tell me about them," he said.

"Not here. Come to my house tomorrow morning."

"I can't wait until tomorrow," he said.

She smiled up at him as he leaned in close. The hardness of his body was a remembered thrill. "We already did lust. Remember?"

"Yes," he said. "I know you remember, too. It's there in your eyes when I hold you. You still want me."

She did still want him, but she liked to think she was older and wiser. Please, God, let her be wiser. She couldn't fall for him again. Wouldn't let herself be that weak where he was concerned. Cam Stern wasn't the kind of guy she could have a one-night stand with and walk away from.

But that was what she wanted. She wanted to pretend they were strangers with no baggage or no commitments. That they could have one night of passion with no consequences. But it was too late for that. She was emotionally entangled with him, even though he wasn't with her.

She went up on her tiptoes and rubbed her lips over his and then slowly opened her mouth and kissed him.

She held on to his shoulders and felt his mouth move against hers. He parted her lips with his own, and his tongue snaked over her teeth into her mouth.

His thrusts were light and teasing, making her crave so much more of him. She opened her mouth wider, held on to his shoulders and let everything drop away. She didn't think about the past or her secrets. She didn't think about the glittering people at this charity ball. She didn't think of anything except Cam Stern and his mouth.

That oh-so-talented mouth that was moving over hers and making her forget everything except the way he tasted and the way he felt.

His lips were firm but also tender against hers. His hands smoothed their way down her spine. One sprawled in the middle of her back and the other dipped lower to her hips, drawing her closer to him.

"Let's get out of here," Cam said. "We need to go someplace private."

Confused for the first time in a very long time, Becca really didn't know what to do. So she followed Cam out of the ballroom and onto the street as he hailed a cab.

Cam wasn't ready to let the night end. Seeing Becca again wasn't at all what he had thought it would be.

The April sky was clear, the night air a little cool but not cold when they left the club. Cam had said his goodbyes to Russell earlier and Russell had offered the car, but Cam had turned him down. He liked to do things his own way. He wanted to be in control.

Cam hailed a cab for them and asked to be taken to

his hotel, the Affinia Manhattan, which was a suite-only hotel. Though he'd only been in town for a few days, Cam liked to have room to be comfortable. At six-five, he was a big man, and he didn't like to be in a room crammed with a bed and a dresser.

"I thought you said you only wanted someplace private," Becca said, arching one eyebrow. "Why do we need to go to your hotel?"

"I don't know any other quiet place we can talk." He wanted her to himself. That was one thing he'd done right during their affair. They had spent all of their time together in her hotel room. Having sex and lying in each other's arms. Despite the fact that they were both working hard during the day, the nights had been filled with only each other.

She tipped her head to the side. She studied him, and he wondered what she was searching for. When he looked at her, he saw the same beautiful, sexy woman he'd known two years ago. But she had changed. There was something mysterious about the woman sitting next to him now.

"Okay, we can go to your hotel, but we are getting a drink in the lobby bar."

"Fair enough. I want to take my time and really apologize for the way things ended."

"Apology accepted," she said.

She was a graceful and charming woman, and as she sat next to him during the cab ride, he surreptitiously studied her. Her heart-shaped face was framed by her hair, and her eyes were dark and mysterious in this light.

He wouldn't have thought to look into his romantic past to find a woman to move forward with, but it made sense to him now that Becca was here.

He stretched his arm out behind her and toyed with the soft tendrils of hair at the base of her neck. "Thank you. But I know you like me so I have that in my favor."

"How do you know this?" she asked.

"The way you smile at me," he admitted. "And the way you kissed me."

"That wasn't about you," she said.

"It wasn't?"

"No. It was a gift to myself. A chance for me to taste the forbidden fruit of the past and then move on."

"Why are you in this car with me now?"

"I wanted to hear what you had to say," she said. "I really don't know much about you."

"Or I about you," he said.

"I think men like it that way," she said.

"Men? I hope I'm a little different than every other man out there," he said. "I think I want to know everything about you."

She shook her head. "I doubt that. As long as I have secrets then I will be mysterious and just a little more attractive to you."

"You couldn't be anything less than you are right now, Becca. I want you."

She shook her head again. "I know you do, but we aren't going down that path."

"I can't think of anything except you in my arms," he said, watching her blush.

"Why are you here? You said Justin is helping his fiancée move."

He laughed. "Fine. I will stop talking about your sexy little body for a few a minutes, but I can't stop thinking about you naked in my arms."

"Cam."

"Okay." He knew he was pushing her, but he only had this night before he had to return to Miami. And apologizing for the way things had ended between them wasn't enough to repair the damage he'd done. He wanted her back. He hadn't realized how much until he'd danced with her. Kissed her.

"I'm here visiting Justin and to attend this charity ball tonight. The African Children's Fund was one of my mother's pet charities," Cam said as the car started moving.

"Well, that's nice." She would have liked to think that she'd made a clean break with everything Cam Stern, but she still read about him in magazines, and late at night when she was feeling very alone, she sometimes went on the internet and read about him. She should have realized he'd be here tonight, but honestly, she'd been busy with work, and having an eighteen-month-old kept her on her toes.

"What have you been up to?" she asked.

"I think I mentioned we are celebrating Luna Azul's tenth anniversary. Even if you can't take me on as a client, I would like you to come to Miami. My invitation earlier was genuine."

"Um..."

"Think about it, Becca."

"I'll do that," she said, but she knew the answer had to be no.

"Ten years is a long time," she said.

"Yes, it is. Are you interested in redesigning the new marketplace?"

"Sounds like that will be a fun project. You can email me the details on that."

"Are you really going to make small talk and pretend that a casual business acquaintance is all that we have between us?"

"Yup," she said. "That's all we have."

"I remember," he said. "But I never meant for those weeks to be the only ones we spent together."

"I know you wanted me to be your mistress...I'm sorry I asked for more."

He said nothing and the silence grew between them.

"You travelled a lot for business back then and I expected you to be back in Miami frequently."

"I stopped working for Russell so I wasn't making as many trips to Miami as I used to."

She bit back a sad smile. To Cam she was just someone to have sex with. She'd seen that pretty early on, and while she enjoyed the white-hot passion that flowed so strongly between them, once she'd discovered she was pregnant, she knew she couldn't be with him.

She had someone else to think of...Ty. Her little gift from Cam.

But talking to him made her realize why she'd liked him so much. The truth was, from the first moment they'd met she'd liked him. He was honest and fair and so damned handsome that she couldn't stop staring at him.

Blue was such a nondescript word for the color of his eyes. They were deep blue, the kind of color that she'd seen in only one other place—the azure waters of Fiji. His jaw was strong and well-defined, but it was his mouth that captured her. Those strong lips that felt so soft and so right against her own.

"You're staring at me," he said wryly.

"I forgot how good-looking you are."

That startled a laugh out of him. "Why did you start your own business? Do you like it?"

"I do," she admitted. "More than I expected to. And being my own boss means I can control my workload. You know Russell is a complete workaholic, so if I'd continued at Kiwi I would probably be in the office tonight."

"Very true," Cam said, stretching his arm along the back of the seat. His fingers brushed her shoulder and she glanced up at him to see if he was trying to distract her. But he didn't seem to notice the accidental touch.

Cam watched her carefully, and she hoped that he took her story at face value and let the topic drop. She knew that right now she had the opportunity to tell him about Ty, but she couldn't find the words.

He tipped his head to the side, and she realized that this evening wasn't going the way she wanted it to. She should be home with Ty.

She thought about how scared she'd been the first night she'd brought him home from the hospital. She had always been focused on her career, so she hadn't had any girlfriends to come and stay with her. And every time little Ty had cried, she'd cried with him.

It had been the longest night of her life, and she'd missed her own mom so keenly it had hurt. But then morning had come, and she and Ty had found their own way.

"What are you thinking about?" he asked.

"Nothing," she said. Seeing Cam again gave her a chance to let him know that he had a son. But she had no idea how he felt about family. She knew he didn't believe in love and had two years ago wanted nothing more from a woman than sex.

"Have you ever thought about having a family? Not just your brothers. I mean a family of your own."

This was it. If he said, *Yes, I'd love to have kids,* then she would say, *Oh, that's funny, you have a son.*

"No."

"Why not?" she asked. Already she had an inkling she wasn't going to like the answer. Cam was too much of a workaholic businessman to want a family. He had only had time for the affair with her because it hadn't interfered with his job. And she knew that.

"I had a paternity suit brought against me right as Luna Azul started taking off. The suit was false but we had to go to court and I think that made me realize that having a child was something I wanted to take very seriously. I didn't want to have a child with just any woman."

Becca's stomach dropped, and she felt like she was going to be sick. She wrapped an arm around her own waist and knew there was no way she could just tell

Cam that Ty was his son. In fact, she just wanted to get out of this car and return to her safe little home as quickly as possible.

Three

Cam had a hard time looking at Becca and not touching her. There was something about her that called to him, and he knew part of it at least was the false feeling that they were still intimates. It didn't matter that it had been over two years since he'd last seen her. He wanted her, and it felt to him that no time had passed.

"I'm glad we met again tonight," he said. He rubbed his finger over her cheek. Her skin was so soft that he could touch it for hours.

The cab pulled to a stop in front of his hotel, and he paid the driver before following Becca out of the cab. The doorman held the door open as they approached.

"I have to call for a car now or I'll never get one later," she said. "I'll meet you in the bar. Go ahead and order me a Baileys."

"I'll take care of the car. You go get a seat and I'll be right there."

"I'd rather—"

He put his finger over her lips. They were full, and he was dying to kiss her again. Touching her mouth, he found it soft and even more tempting than he'd expected.

"I said I'll take care of it."

She playfully nipped at his fingertip and then turned and walked away.

He watched her. She'd surprised him, and he reminded himself that a lot had changed with Becca in the last two years.

And he was dying to know more.

But if he was going to build trust with Becca, he needed to respect the fact that she didn't want to be rushed into his bed. So he called for a car, asking for it to arrive in an hour.

He joined her in a quiet area of the bar where she'd found two large armchairs and a small table.

"I ordered you a Baileys, too."

"Thanks. Your car will be here in an hour," he said.

"Great. So what did you want to talk to me about?" she asked.

"Us. Are you going to give us another chance to get to know one another?" he asked.

As she nibbled on her lower lip, he wanted to groan out loud but didn't. He wanted her mouth, and promised himself that before he put her in a car back to Long

Island, he was going to taste her and prove to himself that she couldn't taste as good as he remembered.

"I'm thinking about it," she said at last. Their drinks arrived, and she held hers with both hands. "It's hard for me to just rush into anything with you."

"If we are going to get to know each other, we should talk," he said. "Tell me something about you that I don't already know."

She paused, her eyes darkening.

"I don't like surprises," she said.

"What kind?" he asked.

"Any of them. I like my life to go according to plan. I can adjust and change my plan but I don't want to have to do it too often."

"Me, too," he said. "Though to be honest, usually I just bully my way through a situation until I get the results I want."

"Hence me having a drink with you tonight," she said.

He just smiled and lifted his glass toward her. He took a sip and sat back in his chair.

"Tell me more about why you are in Manhattan," she said.

"Justin and I are exploring the idea of expanding Luna Azul someday. We are discussing eventually opening clubs in other parts of the country. Manhattan is the first location we are contemplating."

"That's a big step," she said.

"It is. And to be honest, I love our Miami locals. But we are ready for it. And now that you and I have reconnected I will have another reason to come up here."

"Cam—"

He shook his head when she tried to speak. "I want to get to know you better, Becca."

"I don't know if that is a good idea. I'm more complicated than you probably have time for," she said. Her eyes had narrowed, and she tipped her head to the side, studying him.

"I know that. That's why… Am I wrong here to think that there is something between us?"

"No. We've always had that attraction that is impossible to resist, but I want more than that. And you don't."

"I'm willing to try it."

"Try what? I had a hard time getting over you, Cam. I don't think I want to take a chance on letting you break my heart again."

"I can't make promises," he said. "But I do know that I want more than a secret affair. Will you at least agree to come to Miami for the Tenth Anniversary party and spend the weekend with me?"

"As your lover?" she asked.

"I hope so. Definitely as my friend. I want to get to know you better. I feel like we have something unfinished between us."

Becca didn't panic. But she wanted to. Cam had no real idea of what was unfinished between them. She knew that he was talking about sexual attraction or maybe the kind of thing that made her tick. And she knew she wasn't going to share too much with Cam until she could trust him.

"I think that isn't going to be as easy as you might think," she said.

"I know it's not. But anything and anyone worth having is worth working to get to know."

She wasn't sure if he'd mellowed or if it was simply that he was keeping the passion that had flared between them the first time under wraps. But talking was making her realize that Cam was a decent man. A man she wanted to know better and maybe a man that she wanted her son to know.

"I agree." She had to find out more about his past. Had to understand the best way to tell him they had a son. "So tell me what kind of woman you would choose to have a child with," she said.

It was the one thing she wanted to know. Telling him about Ty was only the first step—making sure that he treated her son well once he knew that Ty was his was the important part.

"That's a big jump in conversation."

"I know, but I want to know the kind of man you are."

He leaned back in his chair and took another sip of his drink. "I've never really thought about it. My dad was everything to me when I was growing up, and my mother was more concerned with her social position than her children."

"I'm sorry."

He shrugged. "It is what it is. No changing the type of woman she was. But I want to make a better choice than my dad did. I want a woman who will want to be a mother to our children. Who will make them a priority," he said.

His words made her feel better that he was Ty's father. But she still didn't know if he was just paying lip service to the type of man he thought he should be. And to be fair, he probably didn't know either. She'd had similar uncertainty about becoming a parent. She'd never expected to be a mom and had thought she'd have a nanny who took care of the kid all the time. But once Ty was in her arms, she'd realized she didn't want to miss a moment of his life.

She nodded. "I want that, too. I mean in a dad. I don't want a man who is on his BlackBerry with the office while he is at home and supposed to be spending time with the family."

"Good. Something we have in common," he said. "We both think family should come first. That is partly why I wasn't ready to settle down with you two years ago, Becca."

"Life is complicated sometimes," she said.

"Very."

He leaned forward and took her hand in his. "I really do want this to be a fresh start for us."

She was afraid to believe him. She knew that they'd never be able to make a fresh start unless she came clean first about Ty. But tonight she didn't want to ruin the feeling between them. That excitement and hope that came from getting to know someone the first time—for her it was building on the fantasies she'd spun around Cam since she'd had Ty.

She wasn't going to lie; she'd wanted him to come back into her life. She just never thought that he would. And now here he was.

"Why are you staring at me?" he asked.

"I just realized that I like you."

That made him chuckle. "What's not to like?"

"You are autocratic and bossy," she said.

"I think you like that, too. You need a man who doesn't let you ride roughshod all over him."

"Did I do that before?"

"No, but I think I was the exception. You are very used to getting your way," he said.

"I am. I have had to be. Since I was twenty I've been on my own and that means I have to make good choices."

"Have you always made them?" he asked.

She shook her head. "No, but I try not to have regrets. I mean I can't change any decision I made to get where I am today."

That was one thing she'd learned growing up. Her mother had said that everyone makes mistakes. A wise person learns from them and moves on. A fool lingers over them and spends all their time wishing they'd done something else.

He lifted his glass. "A toast to knowing what you want, and getting it."

"A toast," she said.

He looked at her as if she was the very thing he wanted. That made her feel warm all over, and she knew no matter how hard she tried to keep this tame, it wasn't going to work. She wanted Cam. He was everything she liked in a man. She loved his height; he was taller than she was, with big shoulders and firm muscles. She remembered the way they'd fit together when they'd made love, so perfectly, and she wanted him again.

It had been a long time since she'd slept with a man—since Cam to be exact—and she felt overdue. But a one-night stand wasn't the answer.

"I have a confession to make," Cam said.

She didn't want him to tell her anything else. She just wanted this hour to pass and for her to get into the car and drive away. And this time she hoped that they'd stay apart because the more time she spent with Cam, the more she realized that she missed having a man in her life. Missed having this man in her life.

"And that is?" she asked.

"I'm going to kiss you before you get in the car tonight," he said.

She shivered, and everything feminine in her came to attention. She wanted to feel his big strong arms around her again. Wanted him to hold her and make her feel like she wasn't alone in the world.

"I was planning to let you," she said because she didn't want him to get the upper hand. And because it was the truth—other than the one big lie, she was going to be honest with Cam.

"I thought you wanted to start slow," he said.

"I do, but denying there is lust between us is silly. I want you and I suspect you are very aware of it."

"I am. But I don't want you to feel pressured," he said.

And that made her heart melt. That one comment

made her realize that Cam was a man that she wanted not only in her bed but also in her life.

The driver of Becca's car sent Cam a text when he was outside the hotel.

"Your car is here," Cam told Becca.

"So soon? I really enjoyed talking to you tonight. I'm glad you insisted we get together."

She sounded so casual, as if they were old friends and not old lovers. He knew that was the only way to be unless they wanted to rehash every moment that they'd been apart.

"Me, too," he said. He had enjoyed talking with her. She was intelligent and well-spoken and not afraid to laugh at herself. "I'm going to insist we have breakfast together as well, and then we can discuss business. If you can't help with the Mercado, I think that the Manhattan club will be right up your alley."

"It might be," she said, getting to her feet. "If we have breakfast it will have to be at my place. I hate the morning drive to the city."

He laughed. "Very well. I will come to your place. Give me your address."

She gave it to him as he led the way through the lobby. But instead of taking her out the front door, he pulled her down a hallway to a small intimate alcove.

"I don't want to say good night in front of other people." He put his hands on her waist and drew her into the curve of his body. She fit next to him like a puzzle piece that had found its mate.

"Why not?" she asked, tipping her head back to look up at him.

"I told you I'm going to kiss you, and some things should never be done in public."

He pulled her closer. "That was one thing we did right the first time, kept this private."

She stared up at him. Her eyes were wide and pretty, but he thought he also saw some trepidation in them.

"I agree there. I don't like everyone to know my business," she said.

He stroked his finger over her cheek and then traced her bottom lip with it. She opened her mouth and the tip of her tongue brushed his finger. Everything tightened in his body, and he leaned down, rubbing his lips back and forth against hers before gently mingling his tongue with hers.

She tasted just as good as he remembered, her mouth hot and moist. The Baileys they'd drunk flavored the kiss, but it was the taste of Becca that was addictive.

She moaned deep in her throat, and he tilted his head to deepen the kiss. He was starving for her and was only just realizing it. Letting her go had been a mistake.

He reached down her back and spanned her small waist with his hands, lifting her off her feet towards him. The small mounds of her breasts rested against his chest.

She pulled her mouth away. "I think this is getting out of control."

She had a point, but he didn't want to let her go. Not yet. He lowered his head again, and she lifted hers to meet him. Her tongue slipped into his mouth, rubbing seductively against his, and he hardened.

Letting her go was going to be difficult. But he had made her a promise that they'd go slower this time. And he'd keep it, even if it killed him.

Slowly he let her slide down his body until she was standing on her own again. He pulled back and lifted his head.

"Definitely out of control, but I like it."

She rubbed her fingers over her mouth. "I do, too. But I don't want to make a mistake."

"What kind of mistake?" he asked.

She shook her head. "Nothing. So how about nine-thirty for breakfast tomorrow?"

"Sure. But I'm not letting you change the subject," he said.

She bit her lower lip. "I just want to make sure we both know what we are doing."

"I do," he assured her. He took her hand in his and led her back out into the lobby. It was odd to think of the passionate embrace they'd shared happening so close to the real world and strangers.

"You sound confident but there are things you don't know, Cam," she said.

"Then tell me about them," he invited. "I want to know everything this time, Becca. No halfway for us."

"I'm not ready to talk about all my secrets," she said.

"I'm not going anywhere, so when you are ready we

will talk. There are things that take time to find their way out," he said.

"Do you have secrets?" she asked, then shook her head wryly. "Of course you do. You are a complex man."

"Am I? I think I'm a simple man with simple needs."

"And what are they?" she asked as they approached the front door of the hotel.

"Right now, they involve you in my arms. But that's not happening tonight."

"So what are you going to do?"

"I think I'll go to my room and pour myself a drink."

"Drinking is never the solution," she said.

"I know that, but it will take the edge off my wanting you."

"Does that really work?" she asked.

"I have no idea, but I'm going to give it a try," he said.

She turned and then leaned up and kissed him really quickly. Just a brief touch that sent sparks through his already aroused body.

"Thank you."

"For?"

"Stopping and not pressuring me. It would have been very easy for you to change my mind," she admitted.

He knew that, but he wasn't going to say it out loud. "I want more than one night with you, Becca."

She tipped her head to the side to study him. "I hope so. I'm not that temporary woman I was back then."

"I can see that. I hope you will learn that I'm a different man, too. I'm ready to settle down with the right woman," he admitted.

"I'm not sure I'm that person," she said.

"No pressure. I just wanted to let you know that I've changed, as well."

"I could tell right away. No BlackBerry in your hand during dinner," she said.

"With you by my side I'm not focused on work as much as pleasure."

She flushed. "You are very good about pleasure."

"Thank you." He kissed her hard and deep. "See you in the morning."

She nodded and walked to the car. He watched until the car drove away and then turned and headed back upstairs. He needed to know more about Becca but he had to be careful. He didn't want to be the man to hurt her...again.

Four

Becca woke early, as she always had since becoming a mom. She fed Ty his breakfast and then set him in his playpen while she checked her email. Last night she'd managed maybe two hours of sleep. Her dreams had been plagued with visions of Cam. The dreams were an odd mix of passionate embraces and tearful explanations. And today she felt very apprehensive about inviting him to her house for breakfast.

But it was too late. Cam and she had too much between them for her to just let him walk out of her life this time. And she couldn't move forward until he knew about Ty. It was going to be hard…how did you tell a man that he'd fathered a child with you nearly two years earlier?

She hoped he'd be accepting and understand why

she hadn't contacted him earlier, but she wasn't too confident of that.

The paternity suit he'd mentioned yesterday bothered her. She wished she had more time to do some research on it. But when she'd done a cursory search of the internet, she'd found nothing.

She glanced over at Ty and thought about Cam. What would he think of his son? She should just tell him, she thought, now, before things went any further between them. But she was afraid.

And she hated to give up control of a situation. Right now she made every decision in Ty's life. She chose the nanny and the food and when he went to bed. Once Cam knew about his son, everything would change.

Her life wasn't easy, but it was hers. And the choices she made about Ty's upbringing were hers and hers alone to make. She knew that when there were two parents, things could be difficult. Yet it was a dynamic she'd never experienced since just her mom had raised her.

Growing up alone with just one parent hadn't been easy, but it was what she was used to. So once she'd realized she was pregnant and made the decision to go it alone, she'd settled into it very easily. She'd felt she already had the best example of how a mom handled being a single parent.

The doorbell rang and she glanced at the clock. It was nine. It was a little early for Cam, but she wasn't expecting anyone else. She picked up the baby monitor, leaving Ty playing happily in his playpen, and headed for the door. A quick glance out the window confirmed that it was Cam.

She opened the door. He wore a pair of chinos and a golf shirt. He smelled of aftershave and looked well put-together. She felt frumpy in her slim-fitting yoga pants and T-shirt—so not ready to face the world or Cam Stern yet.

"You're early."

"Good morning to you, too," he said with a smile. "I brought bagels and coffee so I hope I will be forgiven."

She shook her head. Cam threw her off balance. Even without trying, he was doing it to her this morning. She needed that thirty minutes to get her mind wrapped around how to tell him about Ty. "No, you're not. I wanted to change out of messy clothes before you got here."

"You look lovely," he said.

"I don't feel it. I should make you wait on the front step but that coffee smells really good."

"Then I will come in and sit in the other room while you get changed." He seemed so reasonable that she started to feel a bit like a grump.

"Sorry I'm being so grouchy, but I am not a morning person. You can come in and wait for me on the back patio while I get changed," she said. She opened the door and turned to lead the way through the house.

"I'll want a tour later."

"If you're lucky," she said. She led him to the back screened-in porch where she had a glider in one corner and a small round table with four chairs. In the winter months she had glass windows installed to make the room usable year-round.

"I will take care of breakfast. I brought everything we'd need."

She thought she was handling the surprise of him very well when one word from the baby monitor shattered her composure.

"Mama?"

"Mama?" Cam asked.

"I...I have a son. Sit down and I'll be right back."

She left the patio and a perplexed Cam and went to get Ty from his playpen. She bent down and scooped him and kissed his little head. She hugged him close and closed her eyes, pretending that the next few minutes weren't going to completely change their world. But there was no denying it.

As they returned to the back porch, Ty became talkative. "Hi, man," Ty said, from her shoulder.

"Cam, this is Ty."

Cam looked at Ty and then back at her. And then back at Ty again. She saw in his face...he knew there was something familiar about Ty.

"Hi, Ty."

Cam turned to face them both and held out his hand. Ty reached for it and tugged on his finger and then squirmed to get down. He could walk and crawl and really liked being independent.

She bent over to set him down, and he immediately toddled over to Cam. He held on to Cam's leg and looked up at him.

Cam ruffled her son's hair. "I don't know if it is

because the last baby I was this close to was Nate, but he reminds me a little of my brother."

Becca felt as if her heart was going to beat right out of her chest. This would be the perfect moment to tell him why. "Well, it's funny you should say that—"

But his phone started ringing, and he pulled the BlackBerry out of his pocket. He glanced at the screen and then back at her.

"I have to take this. Do you mind?"

She shook her head and walked over to scoop up her son. She felt odd. She'd almost told him the most important bit of news he could hope to get and then business—work—had interrupted. Maybe that was a sign, she thought.

"I'll go get changed and be back in a minute," she said, walking away.

She had to remind herself that when she'd considered calling Cam and telling him that they were going to have a child, she'd decided not to because he just didn't seem like the type of man to want a family.

Their relationship had just been something to get them through the hot Miami nights. She knew that she was partially to blame for that. On some level, it had been exactly what she'd needed from him during that time. He hadn't been ready for anything else, and she knew that because she'd bared her soul to him and he'd told her to hit the road.

There were moments when she still wasn't sure she believed she was a mom. She still didn't believe that her life had taken this unexpected turn and she was where she was today.

But she did want a new start. A part of her did want a partner to share the rest of her life with. And she and Cam did have sexual chemistry in their favor. One thing that Becca had figured out about herself over the last two years was that she missed sex and having a man in her life.

She entered her bedroom and set Ty on the floor while she quickly changed into some nice caramel-colored trousers and a light blue sweater. She put her hair up in a chignon after she washed her face and applied her makeup. Looking in the mirror, she thought she seemed normal enough, but inside she was a mess.

She sat down in the large padded armchair in the corner of her room. It had been her mother's, and sitting there often made Becca feel closer to her.

"What am I going to do?" she asked out loud.

"Mama?"

She glanced over at Ty, who was walking slowly toward her, then decided crawling would be faster and dropped to all fours. "Yes, baby?"

"Where man go?"

She bent over and picked him up, holding him on her lap. "He's still out there making us breakfast."

Becca tried to talk in full sentences to Ty even though she wasn't sure he always understood things. She kissed his soft forehead and felt such joy, love and comfort just from holding him. She didn't want to do anything to jeopardize that.

Her own mother had kept her father's identity from Becca until Becca was eleven. But her father hadn't been a very successful man, and it hadn't been easy for Becca to locate him. In fact, she'd searched more than once for him but never found a trace.

And that had left an emptiness inside of her. Something no amount of soul-searching or club-joining could fill.

There had been other kids of divorced parents at her school, but she'd been the only one who hadn't known her father. Heck, she never even knew his real name.

She didn't want that for Ty. Not when she had an opportunity to give him a father—his real father. She'd have to do it, she thought.

She stood up and walked out the door with a purpose. Cam Stern was going to learn the truth about Ty today, and then she'd deal with the consequences because she wanted her son to have everything that she'd never had.

She wanted him to go to good schools and have new bikes and nice friends. But she also wanted him to have a father. To have a man who'd play catch with him and talk to him. And teach him to drive to someday. And she wasn't going to find a better man than the one who had unknowingly sired him.

Cam was still on the phone when she came out of the bedroom but looked up at her when he saw them. He smiled and then wrapped up his conversation. And despite her determination to tell Cam the truth, her determination to ensure that Ty had a relationship with his father, she faltered. Because she knew that Cam would never again look at her the way he did right now once she told him the truth.

* * *

Cam finished up his call. There was no way that Ty wasn't his child. He looked just like Nate and had the same cowlick that Cam himself had. But how was that possible? He wasn't a man who left things like that to chance.

Becca came back into the room holding the baby, and Cam waited to see how she would proceed. He was angry that she'd kept his son from him, but he wanted to hear what she had to say.

"I'm so glad our paths were brought back together. I felt like we had unfinished business after the way things ended," Becca said. "In fact I have something important to talk to you about."

"That sounds very cryptic."

"I hope that once I tell you…there's no easy way for me to say what I have to, Cam. I want you to know that the last thing I ever wanted to do was to hurt you."

"I repeat—that sounds very cryptic," he said. He glanced again at the boy.

"Oh, man, there is no easy way to say this."

"Just do it," he said.

"Yes. Um…sit down," she said.

As soon as he sat down, she popped up and paced away from him.

She shoved her fingers into her hair and pulled. "You're his father, Cam. I got pregnant when we were together."

"What?" he asked.

"You are Ty's father," she said. There—it was out in

the open, and now they could discuss it like two mature adults.

"I don't believe it."

"What's not to believe?"

"We used condoms every time."

"You know they aren't one-hundred-percent reliable, right?"

"Of course I do. But this has never happened to me before, so don't be snarky," Cam said, getting to his feet. He was the determined businessman she'd first met two years ago. A man used to getting answers. A man used to getting his way.

"I wasn't trying to be sarcastic. I just have been struggling to tell you about Ty and it never occurred to me that you'd doubt he was yours."

"That's where you made your mistake. I've had another woman accuse me of being the father of her child."

Becca put her hands up in the air. "I'm not going to argue with you about this."

"Of course you aren't," he said. "I'm not sure I can believe that I have son, but I see the resemblance and I suspected..."

"You do have one. I'm sorry I didn't tell you about him sooner but I never had any idea that you would care."

He turned back toward her, and she'd never seen anyone look angrier than he did. She took a step away from him, but he didn't walk toward her.

"How would you know that?" he asked.

"We weren't in a relationship, Cam. Don't you

remember—my boss didn't even know we'd slept together." She'd been so overwhelmed by Cam that she'd hardly been able to think of what to do. Two years ago...she'd been twenty-five, and no matter how adult and mature she'd thought she was, well, she wasn't. And Cam had made her feel...just feel. She'd had one other lover before him and it had been little more than a rushed coupling in a college dorm room. But Cam was a real man and he'd swept her away.

"Did you tell Russell?"

Becca felt horrified at the thought of her boss knowing she'd slept with one of his friends. She had kept that knowledge very close.

"No. Of course not. I didn't tell anyone. I don't think that Russell even knows I have a son. I told him I was leaving to start my own company. And he was my boss, not my confidant."

Each question was tearing at her confidence. She briefly wondered if she should have just kept quiet after all, then dismissed the thought.

"I got really sick a month after I left Miami and at first I figured it was just the malaise of a broken heart. I didn't realize I was pregnant until a few weeks after I got back home."

Cam ran his fingers through his hair. He was still sorting out the logistics of how things happened. Answering his questions brought back all those feelings she'd had when she'd learned she was pregnant.

"I almost called you. I didn't have any numbers for you but Russell's secretary had your office number. Do you remember her? Lani?"

"Yes, I remember her," Cam said.

"Then you will probably also recall that you were dating her cousin about that time," Becca said. "And I wasn't about to call you up and give you the news that you didn't want. At that point I wouldn't have been able to handle another rejection. It had seemed to me you had moved on."

"I guess it would. I still deserved to know I had a son."

"I know. I'm so sorry that I didn't tell you but I was in a pretty vulnerable state and you didn't seem like a viable option for someone to lean on," she said.

She crossed her arms around her waist and took a deep breath. "To be fair, back then we weren't anything but lovers. We didn't know about each other's lives or really even care. We just met up each night and had hot sex."

He looked over at her, his large blue eyes unreadable. He seemed so distant and so cold and she really didn't know what he wanted from her. She had no idea what she should say to smooth over this moment.

"That is a fair assessment of who we were."

"Yes, it is."

"Why did you decide to tell me now?" he asked.

She bit her lower lip and fought to find the right thing to say. "When I saw you last night, I realized I owe you the truth."

She was in an indefensible position. She knew what she'd done was wrong and there was no way to spin this. No way to turn it into anything other than the painful truth.

"Now I'm not sure what I believe. But I'm going to take your word that Ty is my son because I can't figure out why you'd make that up. Unless you thought you could get money from me?"

"Why would I need money from you?" she asked. Granted, she wasn't a millionaire like Cam, but she owned her own home and her business was doing very well.

"Everyone always needs more money," he said.

"I'm seeing a side of you I don't particularly like," she said.

"I could say the same. What kind of woman waits until her son is almost two years old to tell the father about him?" he asked.

"I just explained that to you," she said.

"I'm not buying it, Becca," he said. "I'm not buying into any of your act anymore."

"Stop talking to me like that," she said. "You are angry and you have a right to be, but you are just saying mean things right now."

"You're damned right I am. And I have a lot more that I'm trying to hold back. Nothing about this morning has done anything but make me doubt every word you've ever said."

"That's fine with me, Cam. Why don't you leave and we'll never have to see each other again?" she said. She marched over to the door and opened it.

But Cam shook his head. "I'm not leaving yet."

"Oh, I think you are," she said. "I don't care if we ever see you again."

"Sit down, Becca. We're about to come to an understanding and I'm not leaving here without my son."

Cam had never expected to hear anything like the news Becca had just delivered. He let anger roil through him because if he had a chance to think, he was going to be hurt and upset. Two emotions he wasn't about to let her know she'd caused.

"The first thing we will do tomorrow is to find a doctor who can do a paternity test."

"Why? I just told you that Ty was your son."

"I want an official document saying he is and then we will modify the birth certificate so that my name is on there," he said. Now that he was pushing aside the anger, there were a lot of housekeeping items that had to be tended to if they were going to sort out an arrangement for Ty that would ensure his welfare.

"Okay, I can see why you'd want that," she said.

"Good," he said, but he didn't care if she agreed or not. He had rights, and since she'd hidden his son from him since his birth, Cam intended to make up for lost time.

"Next up we will see my attorney and he will draw up papers for us to have joint custody. There will also be an agreement that states that none of my holdings or fortune will fall to you."

"Fine," she said. "This isn't about me, Cam."

He nodded. "That just leaves the matter of Ty moving down to Miami. I can't live in New York and I want my son with me."

"Wait a minute. I'm not ready to move," she said.

"Too bad. You and Ty are going to move down this week and you will live with me at my house. He needs his mother nearby to make this adjustment easier."

"What will I do there? My business is here."

"You will design the Mercado interiors for me."

"Are we going to get married?"

"Hell, no. I'm not about to repeat my father's mistake and marry a woman who puts her own needs first."

"That's not fair. I put Ty's needs first," she said.

"I will give you that," he said. "I have to make a few calls. Pack whatever you need for the next few days and we will leave on my private jet to Miami."

"I can't move that quickly."

"You don't have a choice," he said. "Either you do this or I take Ty and you never see him again."

She was shaking, and tears glittered in her eyes, but she still wore that determined, stubborn look. He knew that he was making her mad, but he didn't give a damn. He'd never felt as betrayed as he did at this moment.

"I will do the paternity test and I will agree to joint custody, but Ty will continue to live with me in New York. You can see him on the weekends if you'd like. But you aren't taking over his life or dictating to me about mine. If you'd been a different kind of man over two years ago, you wouldn't be so shocked now that you have a son."

"I'm not arguing with you about any of this. I know what I want and I will get it. You are welcome to hire an attorney and have him deal with mine. But my son is coming with me now."

"Fine, I will do that. I think it's time you left," she said.

"I'm not leaving without you and Ty. I can't trust you not to sneak off," he said.

"Of course you can. I wouldn't have told you about your son if I didn't mean for you to have a chance to get to know him."

"As noble as that intention is, Becca, it is too little, too late."

She just shook her head. "That's fine. I don't want to move, Cam."

"Too late," he said. "My life is in Miami and Ty's will be, too."

"I'm not giving up my son."

"Then go get packing. My secretary will arrange for movers to come and get your stuff."

"I will need to be here."

"That's your choice but you must know Ty will be staying with me."

"Dammit, Cam."

"Yes, dammit, Becca. How could you not tell me we had a son?"

"You told me I was mistress material and nothing else," she said. "Do you remember that?"

He did, but that didn't change the fact that she'd hidden Ty from him.

"I am not leaving until the movers have been called and I have a chance to talk to them. I will go to Miami with you but I'm not going to allow you to put me and Ty second in your life. If you want to be a father to him, then he deserves the best."

"What do you mean?"

"You can't be a workaholic and a good father. I understand you want to punish me but I won't let you punish your son."

Her words made him realize she was different than his mother had been when it came to her son. "I will be happy to put Ty first. Go pack up what you need. I will call a mover and get someone out here."

He stopped as it finally hit him. "Oh, my God, I have a son."

"Yes, you do," Becca said.

He ignored her and went over to Ty, who was playing happily with his toys. He stared at the boy, and Ty smiled up at him. Then Cam reached down and rubbed his finger over that soft cheek of his.

"My son," he said softly.

He stood there looking at the boy, and the anger that had been riding him since Becca made her announcement started to ease. He could never be mad at Ty or do anything that would jeopardize his son's happiness.

He looked over at Becca. "Why did you name him Ty?"

"It was my mother's father's name. I never knew him, so it seems silly to say he was my grandfather. His name is actually Tyler Cameron Tuntenstall."

"You gave him my name?" Cam asked.

"Yes. I...I knew someday he'd ask about you and I wanted him to have a connection. I know you think this is all some kind of conspiracy against you, but I made the only choice I could for my son. It was hard for me because I didn't want to follow in my mother's footsteps. I had promised myself that my children would have both a mother and a father."

Later maybe he'd be able to appreciate those words, but right now he couldn't. "I didn't think it was a conspiracy. I'm beginning to think it was pure selfishness on your part."

Cam turned and walked out the door without looking back. He knew she wasn't going anywhere in the time it would take him to line up a mover. Right now he needed some space. She'd knocked him for a loop, and he had no idea how he was going to recover. He only knew that his heart hurt.

Less than eight hours later Becca was seated on Cam's private jet and waiting for takeoff. Ty was seated next to her, his favorite stuffed animal—a yellow dog—and his blanket tucked close to him. He hadn't seemed too traumatized by today's events, and she had the feeling that he'd settle in to living in Miami more easily than she would.

Cam had arranged for a mover to get the stuff necessary for her and Ty to live in Miami. The rest of her belongings would be staying in the house. She had no idea what kind of strings he'd pulled, but the men had actually been at her house today and she'd told them what had to be boxed and moved. Her nanny, Jasper, would oversee the movers from here and in less than a week her belongings would be in Cam's house in Miami.

He sat across the aisle and hadn't said more than

two words to her since they'd gotten on the plane. The gentle lover of last night was clearly gone, and she had no idea how to reach him again. But she did know if she was going to move to Miami with her son, she wanted at least a shot at some kind of real relationship with Cam.

She wanted that picture-perfect family she'd always fantasized about. She knew she should try to break the ice but talking to him about Ty wasn't the way. Cam had demonstrated he was too volatile where their son was concerned.

Once they were in the air and could get up and move around, she took off Ty's seatbelt, but he was sleepy and nodding off in his car seat.

"There's a bed in the back," Cam said. "I can lay him down."

"Um...let me see the bed. We'll probably have to pile up some pillows around him. I don't want him to fall off."

Cam nodded. She reached over to unlatch the car seat and Cam was waiting right there. "I want to carry him."

"Of course," she said. Cam had been like this all day. He was genuinely trying to get to know his son, and she had been very careful to let him.

Cam lifted him, and his blanket fell to the ground. Becca picked it up and then followed them to the bed at the back of the jet. It was luxuriously appointed and very comfortable-looking. He laid Ty in the center of the bed, and they worked to put some pillows around him so he wouldn't roll off the bed.

"I am amazed that I have a son," Cam said.

"I am, too. He's such a precious little gift. I...my life changed the moment he came into it."

"I bet it did," Cam said.

He moved to leave the bed area, and she followed him. The jet pitched as they hit a pocket of turbulence, and Becca fell forward into Cam. He wrapped one arm around her as he fought to find his balance and keep them both on their feet. When the plane steadied, she looked up at him and he was staring down at her.

"Thank you."

"No problem," he said, but he didn't let her go. "I can't believe we are in this situation, Becca."

"What situation?" she asked. "Being parents?"

He shrugged. "That, but also moving in together. I still want you."

"I think we need to figure out how to be parents before we do anything else," she said.

"I would agree except for a pressing problem," he said.

"And that is?"

"I can't look at you without wanting to kiss you and make love to you. I want to strip you naked and take out all my frustrations over your actions on your lovely body."

"Sexual revenge?" she asked. His words thrilled her, sent molten heat pooling between her legs and made her nipples hard. She'd be lying if she said she didn't want Cam. That he wasn't the only man she thought of night and day.

"Yes," he said.

She shook her head. "Would you forgive me if I gave in?"

"I don't know. I think so."

She didn't know if she could do what he was asking. Being in his arms was one thing; knowing he wanted her just as some sort of way of getting back at her...well that wasn't exactly what she was into.

"Think about this," he said, lowering his head. His mouth took hers slowly and gently. She felt the warmth of his breath over her lips and then the first foray of his tongue rubbing over hers. His hand tightened on her waist and the other one went up to the back of her neck.

His fingers tunneled through her hair, and he held her head firmly in his grip as they continued to kiss. She wanted to think that this wasn't making her agree with his idea, but it was. It reminded her of how long it had been since she'd had a lover. And she wanted him; she wanted release.

She put her hands on his shoulders and slid them down his arms. He was strong and muscled, and she liked the way he felt under her touch. She continued touching him, finding his belt with her fingers and caressing her way along the edge of his waist to the center of his pants and the belt buckle. She tiptoed her fingers lower until she felt the hard ridge of his erection. She rubbed him through his pants, up and down until his hips canted toward hers.

He lifted his head and stared down at her. His eyes narrowed, and the flush of desire burnished his cheeks.

"Let me know what you decide," he said and walked back to his seat.

Becca stood there aching, wanting, and realized that Cam was still angry at her. She slowly walked to her seat and sat down, taking a magazine out of her bag. She flipped through it but didn't see the pictures or articles on the pages. She only saw herself and Cam, and she knew that if they were going to have a chance at a future together, one of them was going to have to bend. Was it going to be her? She wanted so badly for Ty to have everything she never had, and that included the family of her dreams. One with Cam.

Five

They arrived at Cam's house safely in the early evening. The drive was quick. The estate sat back from the road at the end of the palm-tree-lined drive. The yard was lusciously landscaped with blooming trees and perfectly mowed emerald-green lawns. The building itself was something out of a design magazine, and made Becca feel a bit like she had when she'd met Amelia. Out of place. She liked it, but it didn't look like somewhere she would live.

As she went in, she glanced around the high-ceilinged arched entryway and let out a low whistle between her teeth.

"Nice digs."

"Thanks," he said. She'd put Ty down, and he was

crawling toward the living-room area. "I will show you both to your rooms."

The little boy toddled over and tugged on his pant leg as he had earlier, and this time, Cam bent down and picked him up.

"Hello, there," he said to Ty.

"Hi," Ty said before putting his thumb in this mouth. He shook his head; Nate used to do the same thing when he was little. Cam's memory of that time was a little fuzzy, but this boy reminded him very strongly of his brother.

"How am I going to convince your mommy to just do what I want her to?" he asked Ty.

"Coffee," Ty said.

Cam lifted one eyebrow at the boy. Did he even understand what was being said? Cam suspected he did to a certain extent, but having a conversation with an eighteen-month-old wasn't going to give him any answers to Becca.

The boy held on to his shoulders as Cam turned to face Becca. There was something sweet about holding a baby—his son.

"I'll take him."

She held her arms out, but Ty didn't make any move to go to her. "Ty."

The boy took his thumb out of his mouth. "I like the man."

"I'm glad," she said, taking him from Cam and putting her son on a blanket where she'd laid out a couple of toys. She took Cam's hand and led the way to the hallway where they could still see Ty but he couldn't see them. "I...I wanted to talk to you."

"What about?"

"I..."

"Stop hesitating. You are a woman who knows her mind," he said.

"You have shaken me. I didn't expect to see you or tell you about Ty. Not like that. And then you kissed me and got me all hot and bothered but you want to make it about revenge and I'm not sure that's healthy for me."

"I think it would be excellent for me," he said. "But I am willing to talk to you about this. I'm still so angry, Becca."

"I get that. But we need—"

She glanced over at her son. And he saw the biggest change in Becca compared to the woman she was over two years ago. She had someone else to worry about when she made decisions.

"Is it because of the paternity suit that you're so bitter?" she asked.

"Not at all. I'm mad at you and you alone, Becca," he said. "You owe me an apology after the secret you kept from me. But if you choose to beg forgiveness in my bed, I won't complain."

She nodded. It was a moment of truth for them both. The chances of them changing each other's minds and actually getting to the point where they could trust each other were slim. He wasn't going to deny it.

"Don't judge me too harshly. I never knew my father. He left before I was born," she said.

"I'm sorry. My dad was the greatest influence on my

life. My mother wasn't very maternal, but my dad…I think you missed something really important there, Becca."

"I know I did. And I don't want Ty to grow up the same way," she admitted.

"I'm not making any promises," Cam said. "But you and I had something electric and I think it's time we explored it more fully."

His phone rang.

"Stern."

"Cam, it's Nate. I'm glad you are back because we have an emergency at the club. Some of the local leaders are raising a stink about the Mercado again. Can you get down here and handle it? I'm supposed to be upstairs with Jen practicing a waltz for our first dance for the wedding."

Jen was Nate's fiancée. Cam's little brother had fallen in love with the dance instructor at Luna Azul, and they were planning a wedding in less than a week's time. Love had hit Nate hard and Cam had a little bit of trouble believing it. But his brother had never been happier and Cam wished him the best.

"I'm on it. You go do your dancing thing. I'll be there in less than thirty minutes."

"Thanks, bro, you're the best. I want to hear all about the trip."

"I'll be happy to tell you about it later. Bye, Nate."

He turned to Becca. "I'm needed at the club. We can continue this discussion later."

"It's fine."

"Good," he said. "Becca, I know I said I'd put Ty first...not be a workaholic, but this is an emergency."

"I get that, Cam, but you said that family was important and we've just gotten to your house."

"In the future, I will be here more often. This is an emergency."

"Okay, but I'm not going to let you do it too often," she said, relenting.

He tipped his head to the side. He was still angry she hadn't told him about Ty, but he could see that she wasn't going to be resentful toward him about his work. "Thank you."

She just nodded. He pulled her into his arms.

She flushed and felt the stirring of desire deep inside her. She put her hands on his shoulders, then wrapped her arms around his neck. She lifted herself toward him. He rubbed his hands down her back, cupping her butt and bringing her closer to him.

She felt his erection nudging at the bottom of her stomach and looked up at him. It was a powerful feeling to know that she could make Cam react.

She leaned up to kiss him, but he controlled the embrace. His mouth moved over hers, and no matter how hard she tried to deepen the connection he wouldn't let her.

"Kiss me," Cam said.

She shook her head. "I want you to kiss me. I want to know that there is still a spark of something that's not motivated by your need for vengeance."

"Not yet," he said, rubbing his lips lightly over hers. "I want to make sure you really want me—and not just to get me to forgive you. You do want me, don't you, Becca?"

"I do," she said. "My entire body is vibrating waiting for your kiss. I hate to admit this but I've thought of you and our time together often in the last two years."

"Why do you hate to admit it?" he asked, stroking his thumb back and forth over the base of her neck.

"I think it makes me seem weak and gives you an advantage over me," she admitted.

He cupped her face with his big hands and leaned forward to kiss her so tenderly that she almost melted on the spot. Her knees weakened and her heart beat even harder in her chest.

"I will take any advantage I can get," he said.

He angled his head to the left and kissed her again. This time it was more passionate. He thrust his tongue deeply into her mouth. She shifted in his arms, holding on to his shoulders as he ravaged her mouth.

She wanted more from him. His tongue couldn't touch her deeply enough. She was aching for his weight to be more solidly against her. For his erection to be pressed against the apex of her thighs where she was so empty and needy. Her dreams of Cam had fed her libido for the entire time she'd been pregnant, when her hormones had been out of whack and she'd needed a man.

Now Cam was here and this was everything she remembered. The feel of him pressed up against her made her desire him even more. She wanted to touch his flesh, not feel him through his clothing. He shifted around until the wall was pressed against her back and he was pressed against her front. She lifted one leg and wrapped it around his hips.

He moaned and thrust his hips toward her. He rubbed himself along her pleasure spot until she thought she'd go insane from longing. She tunneled her fingers into his hair and held him to her as his mouth continued to taste hers.

He pulled back, breathing heavily. "I have to go," Cam said. His skin was flushed with desire, and she knew that leaving was the last thought on his mind.

She nodded and turned around to go get Ty. When she brought him back, Cam gave Ty a kiss on the head. His hands brushed Becca's and their eyes met. She said nothing as he walked down the hall and out the door.

Ty was the one man she could trust in her life. It was something she'd do well to remember; otherwise she was going to end up letting Cam Stern break her heart again.

Cam drove through the rush-hour traffic in Miami. He'd taken his new Tesla sports car and wanted to let the car run full out but knew better. He was the responsible Stern, the one who kept his own wants and desires well-hidden from the world, and he sure as hell wasn't going to let Becca change that.

He realized this wasn't the kind of car a family man should have. Hell. He was a dad. He'd had no way of planning for this. It was the one eventuality he *hadn't* planned for. He knew he could do it—he'd raised his brothers and given them a secure platform to launch from when their parents had died.

He'd do it for Ty. He knew he could be a good dad. But he had no idea what to do with Becca. She was the fly in the ointment of his plans for the future.

There was no discounting the sexual attraction between them, and he wished he could honestly say that he only wanted her in his bed…but he knew that he wanted her in his life. He really liked her as a mom. He knew that there were women who loved their children and would put them first. But this was the first time he'd actually encountered one. Then again, Becca had always been different. When their affair had ended, he'd felt her absence in his life. He'd wanted to somehow reconnect with her but…had been afraid of an emotional commitment. That had come back to bite him in the ass—now he had a son and a woman he wasn't sure what to do with in his life.

He pulled into the parking lot at Luna Azul and got out of the car. He walked toward the building and felt that sense of home he so often experience here. This was the place he'd poured all of his dreams and desires into. And the club had taken off. It was more than he and his brothers had ever expected it to be.

Luna Azul was in the heart of Little Havana right off Calle Ocho. It had been a cigar factory in its heyday but had closed and fallen into disrepair when Cam had found it and purchased it for a very good price. He'd decided to make it the premiere club in Miami and had done just that, transforming the former cigar factory's entryway with a Chihuly glass sculpture installation of the night sky showing two moons—a blue moon. And then decking out the rest of the club all in dark Latin tones. Upstairs there was a rooftop club that echoed the streets of Havana back in their pre-Castro glory days.

Now he knew he had to find something else to pour his energy into and Justin had suggested a club in Manhattan. Nate liked the idea because the A-listers there were more accessible than other areas of the country, but Nate had said he'd make it work wherever they wanted to open their new club. He had to think through he details, and he would need to start putting together a team to bring the project to life. They'd all agreed that another Luna Azul wasn't exactly what they wanted. They needed to make that club unique from the one in Miami.

Opening a club was time-consuming, which was why he'd always been into short-term affairs. He'd had to raise his brothers and he hadn't had for another emotional commitment.

"You look very serious, bro," Nate said, coming up behind him and patting him on the shoulder. "Don't worry. I calmed down the local leaders over the latest Mercado drama. We have a meeting set for tomorrow."

Cam turned and gave his brother a quick hug. "I'm glad. I'm thinking about the new club idea."

"Good," Nate said. His brother looked like he'd stepped off the pages of *GQ* magazine, which was why he was the public face of the company, the one who always showed up in the tabloid gossip columns. "What are your thoughts?"

His ideas were rough, but they were starting to take form. He needed something different. The club scene in

New York was just as competitive as in Miami, maybe even more so, and they'd need to be different to stand out.

"That we need something to reflect whatever community we are a part of up there. I was hoping to do something in Spanish Harlem."

"Really? Tell me more."

They'd played a key role in revitalizing the stylized Little Havana area here in Miami, and he was pretty sure they could do the same thing in New York. They just had to have the right idea.

"I know. I was thinking a retro-styled club that captures the glory of the old days. It might fit the city better than a Luna II-type deal."

Nate rubbed the back of his neck. "I like the idea, but it's really different from what we've done before. That will mean a new design team and everything. I think we should stick to doing what we do best and that's a Little Havana-style club."

"I have the perfect designer in mind for this new project. In fact, she's going to do the interiors on all the redesigns of the shops in the Mercado."

"Of course you know the perfect person. Cam, when are you going to realize that life isn't perfect? You always have every angle covered," Nate said.

Cam tried to always appear to his younger brothers as if he had it all together. It was easy enough when things were going well as they had been for the last few years. But when the company had initially struggled or when their parents had died and Cam had had to find the strength inside himself to step up and keep his brothers focused and happy, it had been hard.

"I try, but Nate, I know that life isn't perfect. We grew up in the same house, didn't we?"

"Yes. And I came out of it with my own baggage and lately I'm beginning to see that for you it's a desire to make everything picture-perfect. No faults allowed."

Was that true? "I don't think I'm that difficult."

"Listen, man, I love you. You're my big brother and you always have my back, but you are one demanding son of a bitch and I think that you should accept that nothing is going to ever be as perfect in the real world as you want it to be."

Cam tucked that nugget away for later contemplation. He wasn't going to change overnight or probably at all. He was too set in his ways.

"So who's the designer?" Nate asked.

"Becca Tuntenstall. She used to work for Russell Holloway."

"Are you sure she's the right choice? We don't want our club to look like Russell's." Nate scratched the back of his head. "It's hardly my area of expertise. I just want to make sure I'm asking the right questions now that Justin is out of state."

Justin was their corporate attorney and handled most of the legal problems that cropped up. Recently, he'd negotiated a deal with the local community leaders to launch the Luna Azul Mercado, an upscale shopping center to complement the nightclub. It was fair to all parties involved, and Justin had wrangled himself a fiancée out the deal.

Cam didn't know what was going on with his brothers up and getting engaged.

He smiled at his little brother. Nate had always been the charmer—the one who skated through life with a smile. Now he was stepping up, and Cam was proud of him.

"She's done some work for other chains, as well. She's the best designer for the job," Cam said. He'd already decided to give the assignment to Becca if she proved worthy. He couldn't uproot her life and not provide some work for her. Besides, he wanted her completely under his control. He was going to make her regret not coming to him when she'd first found out she was pregnant.

Nate's expression changed. "Is she more than a designer to you?"

Cam hesitated. He wasn't the type of person to talk about the women he was involved with, even to his brothers. Plus, she was the mother of his child... something that he had absolutely no idea how to tell his brothers. He wanted everything with Becca and Ty figured out and wrapped up before he said anything to either of them.

"Yes, she is."

"Wow. You haven't been seriously involved with a woman since Myra."

Myra had been a mistake, and he'd been too young and too eager to have it all with her. Myra was the woman who'd brought the paternity suit against him. Did he just have bad taste in women or what? Myra had wanted him to pay for another man's mistake, and Becca didn't think he was worthy of his own son.

"She's not really like Myra."

"I didn't mean to imply that she was. How about if you bring Becca to our rehearsal dinner Friday night? A nice casual affair, and I think it would be nice to meet this gal."

But Cam wasn't sure that he was ready for that. "I'll let you know."

"Why not?" Nate asked. "If you are serious about her, I want to meet her and get to know her."

Cam rubbed his hand over the back of his neck and tried to find the right words to say to his brother. "We had an affair a few years ago and it ended abruptly, so this time I'm trying to get to know her more slowly. Listen, there is more going on than a normal relationship."

"Hanging out with the family doesn't seem slow enough to you?" Nate asked.

"I don't know, Nate," Cam said. He stopped and took a deep breath. "Um...I have a son and Becca's the mom. I just found out about it and moved her down here, but I have no idea what we are going to do next."

Now it was Nate's turn to pause. His eyes widened.

"I have a nephew?"

"Yes."

"How dare she keep him from us?" Nate said.

Cam smiled. Nate was always there for him and Justin. They had always been close, and family was more important to them than anything else. "I said the same thing. I have her in my house with my son and I have to figure out what to do next."

"Um, I vote for suing the hell out of her and then cutting her off from the boy."

"She's not like that," Cam said. "Ty needs her. She quit a high-powered job so she could work from home and raise him."

"Damn. I liked it better when I could envision her as the evil bitch queen."

Cam laughed for the first time since Becca had told him he had a son. "Thanks, Nate. I need that."

"I do what I can," Nate said and then pulled him close in a bear hug. "I'm here for you whatever you decide."

None of the Stern men was really built for long-term happiness in relationships. He was very glad to see his brothers settled with new fiancées, but at the same time a part of him feared that it wouldn't last. And he wanted more happiness for them than their father had found in his marriage to their mother.

Cam had been watching after his brothers for so long that it was hard to realize he finally didn't have to really worry over them any longer. He was at a point in his life where he had everything set in motion. Now he could relax.

"How about brunch on Sunday at my place?" Cam said. "I think that will give me the time I need to get used to Becca being there and figure out where we are going next." Then he could control everything if he had them to his house. He was the kind of person who didn't like to be surprised by any eventuality.

He and Nate walked into the club, and, as always when he crossed the threshold into Luna Azul, he paused to appreciate everything he'd worked and sacrificed for to create. Jen was waiting for Nate and came over to them. Cam left them and made his way to the bar on the main floor. He needed to check on the situation with the Mercado and then meet with the head chef and make sure that everything was going well in the back of the house.

He told himself he walked away so quickly because there was work to be done, but he knew that it was really because he wanted what Nate and Jen had. Sure, he already had a son; now he needed to see what kind of arrangement he'd have with Becca. It couldn't be anything as pure as what Nate and Jen had, right? He didn't like himself for thinking that way, but he still felt so empty over the time Becca had stolen from him and his son.

Becca got out of bed in the middle of the night and walked out onto the porch. It was April, and the smell of jasmine was heavy in the air. She walked away from the house carrying with her the small listening unit to the baby monitor. She found a bench nestled next to the pool and sat down.

She knew that, for her, fear came calling in the middle of the night. It was the time when she felt most alone and most afraid of the decisions she'd made in her life. At this moment she felt she shouldn't be here in this house. Coming to Miami had been part cowardice—because she hadn't wanted to stand up to Cam—and part fantasy—because she'd hoped and prayed for some white knight to come and rescue her.

She didn't know if that made her a masochist because Cam was the man who'd left her high and dry. And while he wanted to play up the fact that he didn't know about Ty, in her mind it came down to the fact that he hadn't loved her.

She was here because…she glanced up at the moon and had no real idea why she was here. She felt lost in a way that she hadn't felt since her mother died. Even Ty's presence in her life, as unexpected as it had been, hadn't shaken her the way Cam had. And she had no earthly idea what to do next.

"Trouble sleeping?" The voice was deep and steady. Cam. Of course he'd be out here when she was.

"Yes. I keep trying to figure out what to do next," she said. No use lying to him or pretending a bravado she didn't feel. Tomorrow morning she might be stronger, but tonight she was lonely and confused and needed a pair of strong arms around her to tell her she wasn't alone.

"With what?"

"With you," she said.

"I already told you what I want. I want you. I'm not sure what to do with you once I have you but I know I'm not going to let you walk right back out the door."

"How about if we try to build a realationship together?" she asked. "Something slow where we get to know each other beyond the sex?"

"That won't work."

She couldn't really see his features since he was hidden by the shadows. He stood just out of the light provided by the landscape fixtures.

"Why not?" she asked. She shook her head and leaned forward to put her head in her hands. "I just need time to breathe."

She didn't hear him move, but a moment later his big hand was on her shoulder rubbing in a circle. "I can give you that."

She turned her head to the side and looked up at him. He didn't have on a shirt, just a pair of low-slung pj bottoms. It was hard for her to see him but she remembered that muscled chest with the light smattering of hair. She reached out and touched him. "I've dreamed so many times that you came back to me."

"You did?"

"Yes. It was so hard doing this alone and I wanted to tell you." She started crying, surprising herself with how much emotion she'd bottled up since Ty's birth. "You have no idea...it was only the echo of your words that you wanted a mistress and nothing more that kept my silence."

He stroked his hand over her head and then bent down and lifted her up. He sat down on the bench with her or his lap. "You still should have told me, but I understand why you were hesitant to. I'm truly sorry."

"I am, too," she said, looking him straight in the eyes. She had no place to put her arm but around his naked shoulder, and she did just that.

"I want to start over. But not from a place of anger," she said.

"I can try," he admitted. "But I'm not making any promises. What do you suggest?"

"It's obvious we both want to be parents to Ty. I suggest we try to work and live together for his sake."

"And sex?" he asked.

"I'd like to see it develop naturally," she said. "Not because of some arrangement. Or out of spite."

She held her breath. Hoping that Cam was the man she'd glimpsed earlier tonight while they'd played with Ty and made him supper. Hoping he could see that with all this anger between them, they were never going to be able to move on.

"Okay," he said. "But if you hide anything from me again all bets are off. Ty will be my son alone and you will have no rights to him. I'll make sure of that."

"I'm not hiding anything else from you," she said.

"I'm not kidding," Cam said.

"Neither am I," she promised. She wanted that family of her dreams too much to do anything to compromise it. And if Cam was offering her a second chance, she was going to jump on it with both feet.

He held her in his arms, and they both said little. His hands moved over her as she sat there just listening to the sound of his breathing. She knew that the answers she'd come here seeking were still just out of her reach. But she felt closer to her dreams of a real family and a man who she could trust than she'd ever been before.

When he tipped her head back and lowered his mouth to hers, she knew she should push away and go back inside. She knew that sex with this man wasn't safe for her. But she also knew that she'd been alone too long with only her dreams to keep her company—and that every one of them had been of him.

Six

Becca might need some breathing room, but all Cam needed tonight was Becca. He'd heard her leave her room. He'd put her in the room next to his so he could come and visit her at night once she became his lover again. And he'd had no doubt that she would become his lover. He was determined to have it all this time.

Becca's lie about their son had given him a nice safe place from which to approach this entire relationship. He didn't trust her, and that meant he was safe from falling in love with her. And love was something the Stern men weren't particularly good at. But making love to a beautiful woman—well, that was something else entirely.

And Becca was the only lover he'd never been able to forget. He skimmed his hands down her back and around her hips. He flexed his fingers and squeezed her before moving his mouth from hers.

He nibbled his way to her ear and traced the shell of it with his tongue. "Did you want me on the plane?"

"Yes," she said, her voice light and breathy. "Very much."

"Good," he said, rewarding her with a nibbling kiss at the base of her neck that sent shivers through her body. She shifted on his lap, arousing him even further.

"Have you thought about finishing what we started?" he asked.

She nodded. "But I have to ask you about your reputation as a playboy, Cam. Are you clean?"

That surprised a laugh out of him. "Yes, I am. I give blood regularly. Do you want to see my blood-donor card?"

She flushed. "No. I'm sorry if that made you uncomfortable."

"You had every right to ask," he said. "But tell me, Becca. I want to hear from your lips how much you want me," he said. He brought one hand down low between her legs, stroking her buttocks, and then he lifted her up so she straddled him on the bench.

The fabric of her nightdress fell away from her chest and he had a quick glance of her cleavage. He reached up, cupping her right breast. He rubbed his palm over the globe until he felt her pert nipple blossoming against his hand.

He leaned down and licked her shirt where her nipple was pressed, and she shivered again, her hips moving against his erection.

"Tell me," he said.

"I thought of nothing but that moment and wished you'd taken the kiss so much further," she said. "I want your mouth on my breasts and your hands all over me as I move against you."

Her words enflamed him, and he felt his erection strain against the fabric of his pajama pants. He pulled her night dress up and off her body and stared down at her breasts.

She put her hands on his chest and leaned toward him to kiss him. Her nipples rubbed against his chest, and he felt her rotate her shoulders so that they brushed through his chest hair. He put his hands on her butt and lifted his hips. His erection brushed between her thighs. She moaned and rode him a little harder, her hips moving back and forth without the motion of his hands.

She reached down between them and tried to free him from his pants. He lifted his hips off the bench and reached down to do it himself. Immediately he felt her wet hot core rubbing over his length. He groaned and closed his eyes, hoping to give himself a little breathing room, but he was ready to come. He wanted to be inside the velvet glove of her body. He wanted to hear her breath catch and then make her call his name again and again while he filled her.

"Are you on the pill?" he asked, barely able to get the words out. His voice sounded guttural and deep to his own ears.

"Yes. I am not trusting condoms anymore."

"Thank goodness," he said. He shifted her on his lap

and maneuvered his hips so the tip of his erection was poised at the entrance of her body.

She quivered, and he felt her melt as she started to push down on him. To try to take him. But he wanted to be the one to take her. He held her still with his hands on her hips and pushed up into her one slow inch at a time. She bit her lip and moaned deep in her throat. Her nails dug into his shoulders, and he felt her tightening around him, but he kept his entrance slow and steady. He wanted it to last forever because he knew once he was buried hilt deep, he was going to give in to the tingling in his spine that called for him to thrust into her until he came.

"Cam…."

"Yes," he said between clenched teeth.

"I need you," she said.

"I'm giving you what you need," he said.

"It's not enough," she said, her words like an electric spark in his nerve endings. "I need all of you filling me up."

He groaned her name and stopped torturing them both with his slow entry. Using his hands on her hips, he moved her up and down with a speed that drove them both toward orgasm with no chance to breathe or think. There was only the feel of her nipples rubbing over his chest. The taste of her tongue buried deep in his mouth and the feel of him wrapped so tightly in her sweet center that he thought he'd never want to leave her.

"Cam…I'm coming," she said.

Her words triggered his orgasm, and he pumped once more before he emptied his seed inside of her. She was breathing heavily, and he was covered in sweat as she collapsed against him. He wrapped his arms around her and rubbed his hands up and down her back. He tried to pretend that this was just a little game of getting his own way, but somehow in the midst of seducing Becca, he had been seduced himself.

Cam carried Becca back up to the house and tucked her into her own bed before he left. He wanted to stay and sleep in her arms, but he knew better than to give in to that desire. He walked across the hall to Ty's bedroom and stood over his sleeping son.

He felt as if he'd taken a punch to the chest when he realized that the little boy sleeping there was his. Not just his son, his and Becca's. She meant more to him than he'd ever admit out loud, and tonight had proven it. With any other woman he'd have kept his cool and seduced her on his own terms, but she'd made him lose it.

He leaned down and brushed Ty's hair off his forehead. He needed to make sure that Ty's future was secure. Cam's parents had died in a plane accident so their loss had been unexpected. Luckily, he and his brothers had been in their twenties. But if something happened to him or to Becca, where would Ty be?

He didn't want to take a chance on Ty being left with nothing or no one. His brothers would step in, but they needed to have wills and guardianship issues worked out. He left Ty's room and walked back to his own, hesitating in front of Becca's door.

He wished...hell, he wasn't some wussy guy who

wished for things, he made them happen. So why the hell was it so hard to get Becca to do what he needed her to do? Why was he standing out here instead of holding her in his arms?

Because Becca made him weak. He would never have forgiven a business associate who'd lied to him. And he knew whether he said the words out loud or not, he'd forgiven Becca. He didn't know if it was because of the sex—that would make it easier for him to explain to himself, but he suspected it was because of her tears and the fear she'd expressed so easily tonight. She didn't have all the answers to this parenting thing, and she was feeling her way the same way he was.

He didn't go into her room. That would send a message to her that she had him. Instead, he went down the hall to his office and sat behind his big oak desk.

Worn with age, the executive leather chair had been his father's. Cam had vivid memories of playing under this desk while his father had talked on the phone to his sports manager.

He sent an email to Justin initiating two things. The first was joint custody for Ty. The second was a will that would name his brothers as the guardians for Ty if anything happened to him. He didn't want to leave Becca on her own with no one again. And he knew that she'd never agree to sharing custody with his brothers, but he wasn't about to ask. Some things were just too important to leave to chance.

Feeling better about Ty's future, he got up to go back to bed when he got a text message from Justin.

You have a son?!?!

    Cam quickly typed in his response.

It's after midnight. Why aren't you sleeping?

Selena and I are working. Now tell me I read that email right you have a son?

Yes. 18 months old. Ty Cameron Tuntenstall. Can you do everything I asked?

First thing tomorrow. What about the mother?

She is living with me. I don't know where it will lead.

We need to talk.

Tomorrow or Friday night before Nate's rehearsal dinner party.

Selena's home so I'm going to let this drop until tomorrow. But I want to know what the hell is going on. We'll talk later.

    Cam walked over to the bar and poured himself two fingers of Johnnie Walker, slinging it back in one gulp. He had made mistakes in business and some of them had been costly, but they'd never made him doubt himself the way this thing with Becca and Ty did.

He didn't know if it was simply because he'd never intended to have a family of his own. Or because, having been presented with Ty, now he was starting to rethink himself and his entire life.

His brothers had settled down, and he wasn't sure that he ever would. But now that he had Ty, he sort of wanted to. Becca was an added complication. One he thought he'd have a better handle on if he had her back in his bed.

But sex hadn't made things any easier to figure out. That ticked him off. He poured another glass of Johnnie Walker and sipped it this time, taking the glass with him back to his bedroom. He walked in and didn't bother to turn on any lights. He went into the bathroom and washed up from earlier when he'd had sex with Becca and then padded naked back to his bed.

The moonlight streamed in through the one window blind he'd left open, and he stared at it. His dad had always said that with the moon to guide life's journey, nothing bad could befall them. But Cam knew his dad hadn't counted on a journey like this one.

He walked back across the room, pulled back the sheets and slid into bed.

Becca rolled over into his arms.

"What are you doing here?" he asked her, pushing himself back a few inches.

"I didn't want to sleep alone tonight. I'll do anything as long as you let me stay."

He couldn't push her away. Not when she'd given him the one thing he'd desperately wanted but had been

prepared to deny himself. He pulled her into his arms
and held her close as they both drifted off to sleep.

The next morning, Becca woke up to an empty bed
and quickly climbed out and went back to her room. She
was embarrassed that she'd been so needy last night but
was determined to make today a much better day.

She showered and got dressed and realized she hadn't
heard a peep out of Ty.

She raced across the hall to his room, but the crib
was empty. She hurried downstairs and found the
housekeeper, Mrs. Pritchard, in the kitchen.

"Have you seen Ty this morning?" Becca asked.

"I have. Mr. Stern took him with him to the golf
course. He should be back in about twenty minutes.
Breakfast is going to be served on the terrace shortly."

"Thank you, Mrs. Pritchard."

"No problem. Mr. Stern left word you weren't to be
disturbed."

"I appreciate that. Yesterday was a long day. Moving
is tough work," she said.

"So I hear. I've lived in the same house since I was
born. My parents gave it to me when I got married."

"Really?" Becca asked.

"Yes, dear. They wanted to buy an RV and drive
around the country."

"Did they do it?" Becca asked.

"They sure did. They are still out there on the road.
My dad says he doesn't think he'll get to see everything
before his time runs out."

Becca was touched by the sweet sentiment and

realized how much she'd missed by not having a father. This reinforced her belief that Ty and Cam needed to have a relationship. She took a mug of coffee to the terrace and sat there to wait for them.

Ten minutes later Cam walked out onto the terrace carrying Ty. Cam was wearing golf slacks and a polo shirt. Ty had on a pair of khaki pants and a matching shirt. "Good morning, Becca."

"Mama!" Ty said and squirmed to be released.

Cam set him down, and he toddled over to her. She scooped him up and hugged him close, peppering him with kisses and saying all the silly nonsense she said to him each morning.

"Thanks for letting me sleep in," she said to Cam.

"You're welcome. I figured you needed it."

"I did. Today we need to figure out what I'm going to be working on for you."

"Yes, we do. I think if you come to my office at the club later we can go over it. Ty is going to need a nanny," Cam said.

"Why? I usually keep him with me. I work at home," she said. "If you don't have the space, I can make a corner of my room into a home office. I just need room for my drafting table and computers."

"You can have a home office here, but at times you will be needed in meetings that Ty won't be able to attend with you."

"Good point," she said. "I'll figure something out."

"I took care of it already. Justin's fiancée has a cousin who is going part-time to college and she will be happy to nanny for us when we need her to."

"Us?" she asked.

"We are his parents," Cam said.

It was the first time he'd mentioned being a part of Ty's life long-term. She'd known that moving them here wasn't a temporary thing, but to be honest, she'd thought he'd reacted without thinking through what a life together would entail. And for the first time she saw him as a partner in raising Ty.

"Yes, we are. I want to meet with her before I agree. I don't want just anyone watching our son."

"She's not just anyone. I've arranged to speak to her this afternoon."

"We can do it together," Becca said. She realized, as much as she liked the fact that Cam was stepping up as a dad, she also resented his intrusion into Ty's life. She was used to being the only one who made the decisions for him.

"If you insist," he said.

Mrs. Pritchard brought out the breakfast trays and set them on the table. Ty munched happily on dry cereal on Becca's lap while she picked at a fruit salad.

"Friday night is Nate's wedding rehearsal and then dinner. I am going to bring Ty to breakfast that day to meet my brothers and I'd like you both to come with me to the dinner."

Becca nodded. "I don't have any plans."

"Good, because the wedding is on Saturday and again you are both invited to come with me."

"I'm not sure that's a good idea. Your brother might not want us there."

"Nate does. Family is important to the Stern men

and little Ty is the next generation, so he needs to be included."

Becca hadn't realized how much she'd deprived Ty of. She hadn't just kept him from a father but also from uncles. And in a family as close as the Sterns she knew that Nate and Justin wouldn't look too favorably on her actions.

"Do they know that I just told you?" she asked. Then put her fork down. "Of course they do. What did they say?"

"That I needed to watch my back and they'd support me in whatever course of action I decided to take."

She shook her head. "Course of action?"

Cam leaned back in his chair and looked her straight in the eye. "If I decided to pursue sole custody and take Ty from you."

She wrapped her arms around her son. "Would you do that?"

"No. Ty needs you too much for me to do that. But we had bad experiences with our mother…well, I've already told you about her. It makes them distrust you as much as I do."

"I've already said I was sorry."

"I know. You asked me what they thought of the situation," he said.

"I did, didn't I? I'm just not used to having any family. I didn't think about the fact that you have brothers."

"And I'm getting sisters-in-law, too. Our family is growing a lot, Becca."

"Our family?"

"I meant the Sterns," he said. Cam's phone rang, and he left the terrace to take the call.

She felt left out of something that she hadn't realized she'd wanted to be a part of until this moment. She sat there with Ty on her lap reflecting on how desperately she wanted Cam to be in her family.

Then again, she was going to be thrown into the Stern clan full force this weekend, and she knew she'd better be prepared to deal with hostility and a lot of personal questions. She thought about it for a long minute. Was Cam worth that? Was the chance to make her dream family into a real one worth being grilled by his brothers?

She'd have to wait and see.

Seven

Becca arrived at Luna Azul exactly at noon on Friday. She was still glowing after Cam had sent her a beautiful bouquet of flowers yesterday to celebrate the acceptance of her final design for her hotel project in Maui. She'd finished the job and her clients were very happy.

Cam was the first man she was romantically involved with to send her flowers. It was silly to let her heart melt over it, but it had meant the world to her.

Little gestures like this made it easier every day to overlook the autocratic way he had dictated her move to Miami.

The Florida sun was shining down on her; it was a beautiful April day. Just the kind of day that made her want to skip work and head to the beach or, if she'd been a different type of woman, plan some romantic surprise for Cam. But she had been avoiding any additional intimacy since the night they'd made love.

She stepped inside the club and paused under the blue night-sky Chihuly installation, remembering the last time she'd been here. She shivered a little and reminded herself not to lose her head around Cam the way she had the first time.

"Becca, welcome back to Luna Azul."

His deep, rich voice wrapped around her senses like a warm breeze on a cold day. She turned toward him and forgot to breathe. Though she'd just seen him this morning when they got Ty dressed, it might as well have been a lifetime ago. He had that kind of effect on her.

Cam's light brown hair was thick and disheveled, his features strong. He had that stubborn jaw and those big blue eyes that he shared with her sweet baby boy. He was tall and looked a bit leaner since she'd reunited with him in New York.

"Thank you, Cam." She smiled at him. She wasn't going to let him know how deeply he affected her. But it was too late—he already knew.

He walked over and leaned in to hug her, but she quickly and awkwardly held her hand out for him to shake instead. She didn't think she could handle a hug from him right now. She was trying desperately to be confident and calm and not let her emotions shine through.

But what she really wanted was to run into his arms. To wrap herself in him and just rest her head on his chest. And that wasn't going to happen. She couldn't let what she felt for Cam make her weak. She had to be strong for herself and for Ty.

She didn't want to get too used to having his arms around her, too used to his embrace. It was why she'd spent the last two days in her office buried in work. She didn't want to admit that she wanted him.

"This was a mistake," she said out loud.

He arched one eyebrow at her. "Already. We've hardly said hello."

"Trust me on this. I've got to go," she turned on her heel, prepared to beat a hasty retreat, but he stopped her.

His big warm hand rested on her shoulder, and his body pressed against her back. She melted. That was the only word for what was happening inside her body. Every part of her was enervated and quivered when he lowered his head and spoke directly in her ear.

"Don't go. We are starting over, remember? I'm not going to let you back out on this now. We made a deal."

She turned to face him and realized her error. His face was so close to hers that she was staring into those big blue eyes. His minty breath was washing over her lips, and it was all she could do not to lean over and kiss him.

She stepped back and stumbled. "I can't pretend that we are just doing business together and that you are just another client."

"I'm not asking you to," he said. "I think we made a good start the other night at rebuilding our relationship."

"I do, too. And thank you again for the flowers," she said, finding her equilibrium as her panic eased. "You didn't have to do that."

"Yes, I did."

She was touched. And realized that Cam might be seriously trying to make things work between them. She was, too. And she had to remember that. But all she could think about was his broad shoulders and that the last time they'd been this close, he'd kissed her socks off.

"Come upstairs to my office and we can talk."

She shook her head. "I don't think that is a good idea. You were going to show me the marketplace."

"Seriously?"

"Yes. I can't trust myself alone with you," she said.

He gave her a wicked smile. "Perfect."

"Ha. I came down here to work. I don't want to lose perspective and wake up two days later naked with you."

"I do."

"Cam. I can't do that this time."

"I know we're parents and both busy professionals. But you have been distant the last few days."

"I am worried about facing your family," she said, swallowing hard.

He arched one eyebrow at her again. He was the only person she knew who did that. It was arrogant and right now felt a bit condescending. "There is nothing to worry about. You and I are doing what we can to figure out how to be the best parents to Ty."

He was so wrong, but for this moment she wanted to

believe him. He held his hand out to her and she took it. He led her up the stairs past the rooftop club to a large office tucked behind some rehearsal halls. His name was on a brass plate on the wall. Once they were inside, he closed the door.

"Where is Ty?"

"I left him with his nanny," she said. In the end, she'd needed Jasmine, Selena's cousin. She'd liked the woman, too. She was young and used to being around kids.

"I guess you are wanting to say thank-you to me for finding her?" Cam asked.

"I guess so," she said.

"I think you owe me something for finding the nanny and averting a problem before it arose."

"Like what?"

"A kiss."

"A kiss? I thought we said none of that stuff," she said. "Unless I'm in the mood."

"This is just a thank-you between lovers," he said.

She licked her lips. She wanted to feel his mouth on hers and his tongue thrusting deep in her mouth. She knew the way he kissed. Loved the way his mouth moved over hers and she wanted to experience that again.

"Don't say things like that," she said.

"Why not?" he asked. "Before you say anything else, I want my kiss."

He walked over to her and pulled her into his arms. She knew she should put up some resistance, but she felt safe. As if the past wouldn't hurt them and as if all of her secret dreams were going to come true.

Becca stopped thinking as Cam's mouth moved over hers. He was everything she wanted.

He lifted her onto his desk and raised his head. "That would be a nice kiss if I'd helped you out with something small, but this is a nanny, Becca. I'm giving you the freedom to make your business bigger. I think I need more than just that little kiss."

He was in a good mood, she realized. He was teasing her and playing with her in a way that she knew would make it easier for them to actually build a bond together.

She wanted to argue, but the truth was she also really wanted this. She relaxed and let the material of her skirt slide a little higher on her thighs.

"Come here," she said.

He gave her a wicked grin before taking his first step toward her. He put his hands on her knees and slowly caressed his way up her thighs until the skirt was bunched at her waist. She glanced down and felt a shiver of delight go through her at the sight of his big, tanned hands on her slim, white thighs.

His thumbs stroked both of her legs toward the very center of her, and she felt herself moisten. She shifted on the desk, bringing her hips forward, trying to tease him into touching her where she needed it most. But he kept his touch light and thumbs teasingly close to her feminine mound.

She reached out and loosened his tie.

"No, leave it. I want to be dressed while you are almost naked," he said.

"I'm not almost naked." She squirmed. It did turn her on to have his hands on her while he was fully dressed.

"You will be. Unbutton your blouse," he said.

She reached for the buttons and undid them slowly. His hands moved in circles on the insides of her thighs, and each time she undid a button his thumb brushed over her hot, moist core. By the time all of the buttons were undone and her shirt hung open on her shoulders, she was hungry for more of him.

"Beautiful," he said.

She glanced down at her own body. Her breasts were encased in a pretty, cream-colored lace-and-satin bra. The demi cups revealed the full white globes of her breasts.

Cam moved one of his hands from her waist and tugged at the right cup of her bra until her nipple popped out. She watched his finger move around her areola as his other hand moved in the same circle on her intimate flesh.

"Cam…"

He slipped one finger under the crotch of her panties and his finger rubbed along her lips. He traced the flesh with his large, blunt finger. And surprised a moan out of her when he pinched her nipple.

The two sensations were too much. She felt everything in her starting to tighten. Her skin was flushed, her heart beating stronger and she needed his mouth on her.

She reached for his shoulders and drew him closer to her. He leaned down until his lips brushed over hers. She opened her mouth and felt the hot exhalation of his breath in hers. Then the tip of his tongue touched hers just as the tip of his finger found her opening. He slipped it inside and then back out.

His other hand kept circling her nipple, and she felt the delicate scrape of his fingernail over her as he rubbed his finger up and down.

She moaned and shifted her legs farther apart. "I need more."

He shook his head, his lips rubbing over hers. "This is all you get right now. I want to keep you right here on the edge of desire."

"Why?" she asked, shifting around, trying to make his finger on her intimate flesh touch her harder. She was so close to coming. It would take the barest brush of his fingertip to send her over the edge.

He moved his mouth along her cheek until he reached her ear. "Because I've been like this since I left your house."

He took her hand and brought it to the front of his pants. He was hard, so she stroked her fingers up and down him and then found the tip of his erection through his trousers.

She circled that tip with her fingers until she found the tab to his zipper and slowly lowered it. She reached in to the opening slit of his boxers and pulled him through it. His flesh was hot and hard in her hand, and he moaned her name as she gripped him.

He continued to cup her between her legs, rubbing

along the spot she needed him to, but he wouldn't bring her any closer to a climax. His mouth moved along the side of her neck. She felt the teasing edge of his teeth along that sensitive spot where her neck and shoulder met, and then he bit her so gently that goose bumps spread down her arm and chest, tightening both of her nipples.

He moved lower, teasing her with his mouth. With his tongue he traced the edge where the fabric cups of her bra met her flesh, and the first touch of his tongue on her nipple made moisture pool between her legs.

"Like that?" he asked. His voice was low and husky and arousing. It made her feel very powerful and sexy to be able to elicit a reaction from him.

"Yessss."

He caressed the very tip of her nipple with his tongue circling her flesh until she felt him suck it into his mouth. He suckled her as his fingers moved between her legs. Her grip on his manhood tightened as he drove her closer to a climax. She stroked him up and down as his fingers moved faster between her legs, and then everything convulsed inside of her and she threw her head back and cried out his name.

He still sucked strongly on her nipple as everything inside of her clenched and then released. She let go of him and brought her hands to his head, tunneling her fingers through his thick, chestnut hair and holding him to her.

He lightened his touch but didn't let her go. He turned his head on her breast, and she cradled him to her. It was nice but it wasn't enough. She wanted Cam inside of her.

"What are you thinking?" he asked.

"That I never want you to let go of me," she answered honestly, hugging him as closely as she could.

Cam had put off his pleasure as long as he could. He wanted to have a bond that couldn't be broken.

He pushed her blouse off her shoulders and leaned forward to undo the clasp of her bra. It loosened, and she shrugged it off, tossing it aside.

She couldn't be more beautiful. He ran his hands down her shoulders to her chest and cupped her breasts in both of his hands. She leaned back on her elbows and looked up at him.

It was the most sensual thing he'd seen in his life, and he knew the image of her like this—on his desk—was going to stay in his mind for a long time.

He played with her breasts until she reached for his erection, drawing him closer. "No more games, Cam," she said. "Come inside of me and make me yours."

He reached for her hips and lifted her with one arm while he pulled her panties down her legs and tossed them on the floor.

He glanced down at her almost bare body. She looked so sexy lying on his desk like a feast waiting for him.

She rubbed her finger over the moisture at the tip of his erection, then brought her finger to her lips and licked it. Her eyes closed as she sucked his essence from her finger, and he knew he couldn't wait another second to get inside.

He pushed her thighs farther apart and came forward, poised to enter her. The sensation of flesh on flesh gave him pause.

He looked down at her face. She lifted herself toward him, her mound rubbing against him. He groaned her name. Her breasts jiggled as she moved and he leaned down to take the tip of her nipple into his mouth. He suckled her, searching for something that could only be found with her.

She shifted her thighs, and he moved closer as she wrapped her legs around his waist. He nudged her opening and teased her by slipping just the tip of his erection in and out of her body.

She moaned his name, and he pulled back, looking down at her feminine secrets, which were exposed to him. He traced his finger over the smoothly shaven area.

She reached for his hips and tugged him forward. He entered her slowly at first and then plunged all the way to the hilt. She felt so good, and he told her so, whispering dark sex words in her ear as he pulled slowly out of her body.

Her skin was smooth and smelled of peaches. He just couldn't get enough. He kissed her neck, then licked the skin at the base of her neck.

He was addicted to the taste of her. The feel of her. She went to his head and consumed him. All he could think of was staying inside her body forever. He had it right a couple years ago when he'd taken her to his bed and kept her there for a matter of weeks.

He felt her tighten around him, and he wanted to

get deeper inside. Needed to take her as deeply as he could. He put his arms under her thighs and lifted her legs high, resting her heels on his shoulders.

She leaned back on his desk. Her pert breasts with their berry-hard nipples were tantalizing. He reached down and palmed her as he thrust even deeper into her body.

And it still wasn't enough.

He felt everything in his body driving toward climax. Tingles started to move down his spine as she reached up for his shoulders and pulled him closer to her.

She lifted her neck and shoulders and found his mouth with hers. She sucked hard on his tongue, and he responded by thrusting into her harder until her hips were lifting toward him.

She held him tightly to her, and she cried out his name as she came. He tried to hold on, not wanting to come so quickly, but everything inside of him clenched and he spilled himself at that instant.

He kept thrusting into her and felt her tighten around him again as she continued to come. Then he stopped and fell into her arms. She held him close. For the first time since she'd come back into his life, he felt a moment's peace.

This—she was what had been missing in his life up to this point. And having her again made him acknowledge that it had been a mistake to ever let her go. Becca was his.

"You're mine now," he said.

"Am I?" she asked.

"Yes."

He leaned over her on the desk, keeping their bodies connected. He kissed her softly and tenderly, letting the emotion of this moment overwhelm him. She was more than just sex to him, and he had no words to tell her but hoped that one small kiss would convey what he was feeling.

She wrapped her arms around him and toyed with the hair at the back of his neck. He could rest in her arms for a lifetime.

A lifetime.

She went to his head faster than anything else ever had. He'd always been disciplined, so alcohol and women had never been a distraction for him.

But Becca was.

Looking down at her at this moment, he realized he didn't want to spend another day without her by his side. He wanted to give her things she couldn't give herself.

There was something very rewarding in doing that, and he wasn't about to let her slip away. Or was he? It wasn't just Becca whom he was getting involved with. There was his son to think about.

The son she'd hidden from him.

He glanced down at her. She had her eyes closed sleepily. He knew she wanted to stay in his arms—and he wanted her there. But too much. At some point she'd become too important to him, and that was dangerous. He needed distance.

He pulled back. He wasn't ready for this type of feeling or commitment.

He pulled out of her body and handed her some tissues from the box on the corner of his desk. He couldn't think of anything to say as he turned and walked to his private washroom.

Then he looked at himself in the mirror and knew that no matter how much he wanted to pretend that nothing had changed between him and Becca, it had.

He had no idea how he was going to go back to being the man he'd been before. The man who had a barrier between himself and everyone except his brothers. Damn, she'd shown him that he was vulnerable. Something he'd never wanted to admit or acknowledge before.

But now he wasn't sure he wanted to go back to his old life. And he'd never been the kind of man who didn't know what he wanted. He wasn't going to let Becca slip away, so he had to figure out how to keep her in his arms *and* keep the space between them that he needed for his life to stay on track.

Becca was everything that he needed to make his life the complete package. But he didn't want to lose his head and forfeit everything he'd already worked hard for.

Eight

Becca hopped off Cam's desk as soon as he closed the bathroom door behind him. She found her panties and bra and quickly put them back on. Making love had seemed the right thing to do, but after he'd walked away she felt small and vulnerable.

More vulnerable than she'd expected to. The last time they'd had sex she'd just felt fulfilled. But she knew this time the stakes were much higher. She wanted Cam to be more than her lover. She wanted the little pretend family they had to be real.

She put her blouse on and buttoned it swiftly. She put her shoes back on and stood there for a few more minutes, wondering what she should do. She wanted to leave but that didn't feel right.

It was clear that making love had affected Cam as

deeply as it had her. The thing she didn't know was *how* it had affected him. For her it had felt like the confirmation of everything she'd been longing for. For him…well, she had the feeling that he wanted to pull back and put some distance between them.

She was tempted to leave right now. She heard the toilet flush and realized he was going to be back out in a minute. Was she staying or going?

She started for the door but stopped as she heard him behind her.

"Where are you going?" he asked.

"I wasn't sure you wanted me to stay," she said. What she really wanted—no, needed—was a hug. She needed his arms around her so she wouldn't feel so alone and so damned fragile. But the look on his face said there wasn't going to be any cuddling. Not now.

"I'm not sure either," he said. "I thought that having you would ease the tension between us, but I may have created more problems."

She swallowed hard. "I don't know. I wanted to be your lover and spend every night with you. You were right—living together and not sleeping together is weird."

"Me, too, but we are still strangers. Sexually compatible strangers, but maybe we need to cool it for now."

She nodded. "Um… I need to go home and have a shower before the rehearsal dinner."

"Why?"

"Because I can still smell you on my skin and I need to be thinking with my mind and not my hormones if I'm going to meet your brothers."

"I like the thought of my scent on you," he admitted. "And I want to talk about the Mercado before you go home. If you stay on that side of the desk I think we can conduct business and then you can go home. I will pick you up at seven."

She nodded. He talked about what he wanted for the Mercado, and she took copious notes. When he was finished, he walked around his desk. He turned to the credenza along one wall and picked up a portfolio. "This contains the design specs for our new project. Take it with you and look it over."

She took the leather binder from him, and when their hands brushed against each other, she shivered. She still wanted him. During their affair two years ago they'd spend an entire afternoon making love. And to be honest, now that her body had had him again, it craved more. She craved more.

Why was Cam the one man in the world who could make her feel like a sex-crazed teenager? It had been that way from the beginning, and she shouldn't have been surprised that two years later nothing had changed.

"Why are you staring at my hands?" he asked.

"I was remembering the way they felt on my body," she said.

He cursed low under his breath and put his hands on her waist, drawing her closer. "I was thinking the same thing. This starting over is hard."

"Yes, it is. I wonder if we are making a mistake," she said, tipping her head back so she could look up at him.

She wanted to see a sign in him that everything was going to be okay but his dark blue eyes were unreadable. There was no sign. And she felt foolish for even looking. Since her junior year in college she'd been on her own. Why should now be any different?

She was the one who took care of herself and made sure that she had what she needed. Cam wasn't going to be her hero or her white knight. That wasn't the kind of guy he was.

He was a modern man who expected the woman he was involved with to be her own savior. And it didn't matter one bit that all she wanted was to cuddle close to him and rest in his arms. That she wanted some kind of comfort from him and the assurance—no matter how false it was—that everything would be okay.

"No," he said. "This wasn't a mistake. I won't let it be." He kissed her tenderly on the forehead. "I'm sorry I'm rushing you out the door, but Justin just got back to town and I have a meeting with him and Nate in twenty minutes. You have made me forget about work."

"Oh, okay."

"I had no intention of seducing you this afternoon. But I'm glad I did."

"Are you sure?"

"No. But I don't regret it and I think if we ignored this side of our relationship we'd be starting over on a lie and I don't want that."

She flushed and nodded and walked away without saying another word.

* * *

He felt as if he was missing something important but had no idea what it was and could only watch her leave.

Calling her back to him would be the right thing to do, but he needed some space. Some distance to figure out who he was and what he should do next.

He had never encountered anyone who shook him up the way she did. He wanted to pick her up in his arms and lock the door and make love until they didn't have the strength left to lick their lips. But that wasn't going to happen.

He also wanted to make sure she knew that she was more to him than a lover. He had to keep reminding himself that he was moving on to another stage in his life. But he didn't want to put the white-hot lovemaking with Becca behind him.

He realized that the two of them were always going to be incendiary, and nothing was going to change that. He just had to figure out how to manage that part of the relationship.

Added to that was the fact that they were parents. Ty was important to him and Becca was important to Ty. So they were tied together in way that he hadn't anticipated. A way he'd never been attached to someone before.

He sank back in his chair and tried to concentrate on business. It had never been hard for him until now. He knew where his focus needed to be, but Becca challenged that. He wasn't going to be an absentee father to Ty. Not that he wanted to be but, honestly, he knew more about babes than babies and he was struggling to find his way with his son.

There was a knock on his door and he beckoned the person to enter. It was Justin and his fiancée, Selena. Cam got up and walked over to his brother, embracing him.

"Glad to have you back home," Cam said.

"Good to be here," Justin said.

Cam leaned over and gave Selena a kiss on the cheek. "Have a seat, you two, and I'll tell you about our problems."

"With the Mercado?" Selena asked.

Selena was a beautiful Latina with olive-colored skin and thick ebony hair. She was petite and curvy. And she had eyes only for Justin. Something that always made Cam feel good. He liked seeing his brothers with women who clearly adored them. He wasn't sure if it was because his mother had been so cold or not, but he had never thought any of them would find a woman they could be that comfortable with.

At moments, he thought that he might find that with Becca. But he doubted it. He'd have to relax his guard around her and she'd have to do the same and they were both wary of each other to do that.

"Yes, with the Mercado. We need to close down the businesses while we are doing construction," Cam said.

"I thought we'd already agreed that you would keep them open," Selena said.

Selena had been the big-gun New York City attorney

that the Mercado merchants had hired to represent them.

"We did. But there are safety concerns."

"What concerns?" Justin asked.

"We can repair the sidewalks and redo the facades while the businesses are open. Some of the repairs can wait until we have a new design in place but there are concerns about the cracked sidewalks and the parking lot is a mess. It's not safe to have people in and out of the shops while we have that machinery there," Cam said. He knew that the business owners were concerned about their bottom lines but safety was important, too. They were flirting with a lawsuit if someone got injured during the construction phase.

"I'm sure they don't want anyone to get hurt," Selena said.

"Tomas is stubborn, Selena. Your grandfather argues with me about everything. Even if he knows that I'm not trying to hurt his business, he still has to make me negotiate everything."

Justin started laughing. "I will see what I can do. He is always looking for a little more."

"Yes, that's it exactly. Now that business is out of the way…we need to talk about Nate's bachelor party."

"I think that's my cue to exit," Selena said. "I'm going to my *abuelita's* house, Justin. Meet me there later?"

"Yes. I think we'll be done in an hour or so."

"Perfect," Selena said. "Bye, Cam."

Selena left and Cam was alone with his brother.

"Becca is going to be at the party tonight...I want you to be...well, nice."

"Geez, Cam, I'll try."

"Good. That's all I ask. Nate is stoked about the wedding," Cam said, changing the subject.

"I know. He keeps texting me about what Jen did or said. It's funny, I never saw him as a family guy, but then I never expected him to quit playing pro baseball, either."

"Life has a way of making you change," Cam said. Realizing that life was doing that to him right now. He had to change or lose Becca and Ty.

"Yes, it does. I think I'll walk over and talk to Tomas, then meet up with Selena. Do you need me for anything here?"

"Nah, I'm good."

Justin left, and Cam went back to work on some details for the tenth-anniversary celebration.

When she got back to Cam's house, Becca walked into her room and tossed the portfolio on the bed. There was a note from Jasmine saying that she and Ty were down at the pool. She kicked off her shoes and fell back on the bed. Staring at the ceiling, she searched for answers. Just once she'd like something in her life to go easily.

She wished her mom were here so she'd have someone to talk to. Becca knew that if her mom were alive, she'd have some good advice about what she should do. Her mom had always been a big proponent of truth and consequences. And Becca knew if she'd sent Cam a letter or told him about Ty when she'd first gotten pregnant, she wouldn't be in this predicament now.

She rolled over on her stomach and stared at the luxury room. The scent of Cam lingered on her skin, and the feel of him seemed to be imbedded in her senses.

She got off the bed and went to the bathroom, showering off Cam and what had happened between them. Tonight when they had dinner, she'd see how he treated her around his brothers. She was keen to know if they were really a couple in his eyes or if she was still just his secret lover.

She emerged from the bathroom determined to take control. Since Cam had forced her to move down here, she had to let the situation dictate what she did and how she acted, but now she had be the one in charge.

She took the portfolio that Cam had given her and opened it. Work had always been her solace, and it was now. The design specs were right up her alley, and as she read over them, her mind was filled with visions of how to bring the Stern brothers' desires for the Mercado to life.

She started sketching and drawing and making notes, and when Jasmine and Ty came back from the pool almost two hours later, she had the beginnings of a spec design for Cam.

She stopped working and held her son in her arms. After a while, she sent the nanny home and went to bathe him. She wanted them both to look their best when they met Cam's brothers. She was so nervous, she could hardly think straight.

She smiled, but her heart wasn't in it. This thing with Cam was a black cloud hanging over her. It would continue to be until she knew what it was he intended for the two of them. Would they just continue to live together and raise their son and make love? Or was there going to be something more? Already she felt her emotions building, and she knew she was very close to falling in love with him again.

She looked at herself in the mirror and saw how lost she looked.

"Ah, Becca, don't look so sad. You have a wonderful son and a good life. If Cam is half the man you believe him to be somehow this will work out," she said to herself.

She'd been alone too long, and she wanted what every mother wanted...to have the father of her child in her life and to create a family.

She didn't know if the desire was keen for her because she'd never had that nuclear family growing up, but she knew that it was important to her and she wanted it.

After getting Ty dressed, she cuddled him close to her so that she could find some solace in holding him. And waited for Cam.

Cam showed up promptly at seven to pick them up. Earlier this week, he'd bought a new SUV for them to drive Ty around in. Yet another sign that he was warming up to being a father. Cam got out of the car and took Ty.

"You both look nice. The rehearsal went well and I

think you are going to find my brothers on their best behavior."

"Why?"

"I told them that we were trying to do right by Ty and I don't want them to make you feel uncomfortable," Cam said as he buckled Ty into his car seat.

"Thank you, Cam."

"It was the least I could do. I did drag you down here and install you in my home. It wouldn't be fair of me not to look out for you."

Her heart melted. This was what she'd been waiting for. For the first time since she'd made that decision to let Cam manipulate her into coming here, it felt like the right one.

She leaned over and kissed him hard on the lips. "Every time I think I have you figured out, you do something unexpected."

"Good," he said. He opened her door for her and she got into the car. She watched him walk around the front and climb behind the wheel.

"I never thought Nate would settle down with one woman," Cam said.

"From what I've read, he always did seem to be the ultimate playboy."

"Part of that was for the club. He has always used his celebrity to keep patrons packing our dance floors."

"It's obviously worked," she said.

"Yes, it has. When I first had the idea for the club I never imagined that Justin and Nate would find the work as fulfilling as I did. I really just wanted their help financing the business and an excuse for us all to have to stay close."

"And instead you created the hottest nightclub in Miami and your brothers are your best friends."

Cam tipped his head to the side to stare at her as he braked for a traffic light. "They are. I hadn't realized it until you said that. Who are your friends, Becca?"

She shrugged. "I have some casual acquaintances at the Mommy-and-Me program in Garden City, but I'm really not the type of person who shares much with others."

"I can vouch for that. You are a very hard woman to figure out," he said.

She really wasn't, but she was glad he thought so. She hoped it added to her mystery to have him not too sure of her.

He pulled to a stop at Luna Azul a few minutes later.

"What are we doing here?"

"The rehearsal dinner is at the rooftop club. It's where Nate and Jen met."

"Great. Can we bring Ty?"

"Definitely. Someday this is going to be his club and he should start getting used to the place now."

Cam opened her door before getting Ty out of the car seat. As they approached the club, Cam held Ty in one arm and had his other around Becca. She caught a glimpse of them in the reflection of the glass door as they approached, and they looked like a real family. The one she'd always wanted for herself.

* * *

The nightclub wasn't really suited to kids, but there was a family atmosphere to the rooftop club tonight in addition to Nate's A-list celebrity friends like Hutch Damien, the rapper turned actor, and several New York Yankees players both past and present. Jen had brought her family. And Justin's fiancée, Selena, had brought her grandparents and several cousins.

Nate waved Becca, Cam and Ty over as soon as he saw them. At the same time, Selena's cousin Jasmine came up to them and took Ty away to meet some of the other kids. "You two enjoy yourselves. I will watch little Ty."

"Are you sure?" Becca asked.

"He'll be fine," Cam assured her.

Cam grabbed two mojitos off the tray of a passing waiter and handed one to Becca. "Just be yourself."

"I don't know how to be anyone else," she said.

Damn, if that wasn't true. It gave him an insight into why she was so special to him. But he didn't have time to analyze it.

"Hey, big bro," Nate said, hugging Cam. "I'm so glad you are finally here."

"I am, too. Nate, this is Becca Tuntenstall. Becca, my youngest brother, Nate."

"It's so nice to meet you," Becca said, holding out her hand. "Congratulations on your upcoming marriage. I'm looking forward to meeting Jen."

Nate took her hand and shook it. "I want to know about my nephew."

"Ask me anything," she said. "I love to talk about Ty."

Cam stepped back and watched as Becca did that for about fifteen minutes. It was clear to him and to Nate as well that Becca loved her son.

"Let me go get him so you two can meet," she said.

Becca walked away before Nate or Cam could say anything, and they just watched her go.

"I like her," Nate said.

"Good. I do, too."

"Yeah, I kinda figured that out by the way you keep watching her."

Nate laughed.

"So are you ready to settle down with Jen, little bro? Is the whole domestic routine treating you well so far?"

Jen stood off to the side, talking to her sister and nephew. She was animated during their conversation. She held her nephew's hands and danced to the music with him.

"More than I thought. I mean, I like a good party but I don't have to do a club crawl every night to feel like I'm alive. I get that from Jen."

Cam was relieved to hear that but also a little worried. Nate was the one who made sure that Luna Azul kept drawing the celebrity crowd and stayed in the paper.

"What about our publicity?"

"Don't worry. I've got you covered. I blog from here and already sent in some photos from earlier tonight. And when you guys leave I'll hit Luna for a few minutes before calling it a night."

"That's a bit of an odd schedule," Cam said.

"Yes, but it works for us. Jen likes spending the evening with me."

"That is a very good thing. I wonder what Dad would make of this," Cam said.

"He would probably go running for the hills. As much as he loved us, I don't think this was his kind of gig," Nate said.

Cam looked around the rooftop and wondered if Nate had a point. Perhaps domestic bliss hadn't been in the cards for their parents. But at least their father had loved being a dad. And that was important.

"Are you sure you are ready to tie the knot tomorrow?"

"Positive."

"Good. I'm happy for you," Cam said.

He glanced over to see Becca coming back with Ty. Just then, Cam thought that Ty was going to need some cousins.

He turned back to his brother. "Have you and Jen considered having kids?"

Nate nearly dropped his drink, which made Cam laugh. "I'll take that as a no."

"You just asked me about clubbing—you know a dad doesn't have time for that stuff. And Jen's a dancer, so she has to think good and hard about what she'd be giving up before we even entertain that idea."

"Okay, that's the stock answer you guys give everyone. I'm your big bro, so what's the real deal?"

Nate turned and looked over at his wife. "I've thought about it a lot, but the subject hasn't come up between us. And I don't know if I'm ready, Cam. The last thing

I want to do is have a child and not be the parent that Dad was."

His words resonated with Cam. Their dad had been a great father, and living up to the old man would be hard. But when Cam looked at Becca and Ty, he wanted to be a parent. He wanted to be the missing piece in their little family.

And that didn't fill him with panic the way it once would have. He thought that was a good indication that he was on the right the track with Becca. That she was the one.

"I guess you think about it," Nate said.

"I didn't before Becca came back into my life."

Cam rubbed the back of his neck.

"I bet."

Becca walked right up between them. "Ty, this is your uncle Nate. Nate, this is Ty."

Nate looked down at Cam's son, and Cam felt a moment of familial bonding that until now he never could have imagined. He was glad to see his brother and his son together. And when Nate held out his arms to Ty and Becca handed him over, Cam realized he'd made the right choice in going after joint custody and in naming his brothers as guardians in the will.

"He is so cute," Jen said as she came up to them.

"My brother sure is," Cam said with a wink.

"I meant your son. But I have to agree—my husband is a hottie."

She slipped her arm around Nate's waist and looked up at Cam. He was very happy that his little brother had found a woman who loved him. And that that love was clear for everyone to see.

"I am a hottie," Nate said. "I think the entire world knows that."

She laughed. "Gosh, I hadn't noticed."

Nate kissed her soundly on the lips and then smacked her butt. "Smarty. Everything is almost ready here. Go get ready for our dance."

Jen pinched Nate's butt. "I will but only because I'm the one who thought of the idea to get everyone in the party mood."

Cam laughed at the two of them as Jen walked away. There was something welcoming and refreshing about being in their presence. Nate handed Ty back to Becca.

"I don't pretend to understand what's between you and my brother," Nate said. "But I'm glad you and Ty are here."

"Me, too," Becca said.

"I have to agree," Cam said. "I'm very glad to have you both in my life."

Nine

Becca hadn't expected to enjoy herself as much as she did at the rehearsal dinner. But when the music started and as the mojitos kept flowing, she found herself on the dance floor with Cam.

"This is where it all started," he said.

"The dance floor? We met in Russell's conference room," she reminded him.

"No, that's the past, when we were too involved in ourselves to figure out what was really important. I knew when I danced with you in New York that something had changed. You weren't the woman I had known before," he said, spinning her around as one of Shakira's slow, sexy ballads played.

"I'm definitely not the same woman. It was hard

for me to be attracted to you and know I had a big secret."

"I bet. Did you think about running away?" he asked.

It was the first time they'd really talked about everything, and she was glad to finally have the chance. "For a minute. But I had Ty to think about. And once I talked to you that night I realized there was more to you than just a sexy guy I had an affair with. I'm not sure how to say this, but I think you were right to tell me I wasn't in love with you two years ago."

"You do? Why?"

"I didn't know you at all. If you had taken me up on my offer...we would have been married with a kid and both felt trapped and miserable," she said.

"Or would we have uncovered the truth about each other as we have these last few weeks?"

"I'd like to think we would have, but I don't believe in fairy tales anymore."

"Did you at one time?"

"Yes. When I was young. I spent a lot of time dreaming up where my dad was and making up excuses for why he never came to see me."

"Ah, Becca," he said, pulling her close in his arms. "I'm so sorry."

"It's not your fault," she said. "Life is like that sometimes. Then other times the man who you cursed for being a jerk shows up and turns out to be a hero."

"Me?"

"You."

He leaned down to kiss her. And saw his brother walk up right behind her on the dance floor.

"No need to ask who this is," Justin said. "Your son's mother, I presume."

"I am Ty's mother," Becca said, turning to confront Cam's other brother. "You must be Justin."

"I am. I'm also the family attorney. Did he mention that?"

"Back off, Jus."

"I'd be happy to if I could understand why she kept your son a secret for so long," he said.

"Cam had told me he wasn't ready for a family and I am a loner. I like to do things on my own. That's the only explanation you are going to get," she said.

"That's more than he deserves. I told you not to bring this up tonight," Cam said.

"I'm sorry, Cam. I don't like the feeling that she's trying to pull one over on us," Justin said.

"She's not."

"I'm not," Becca said at the same time. "I didn't trust your brother to be a good man."

"I didn't see it that way," Justin said.

"That's because you are used to seeing the worst in everyone," Selena said, coming up net to her fiancé. "I'm Selena Gonzalez, by the way. You must be Becca."

"I am. Nice to meet you," Becca said, holding her hand out to Selena.

"You, as well. Please excuse Justin. He just—"

"Doesn't want to see his brother treated poorly," Justin said.

"I'm not treating him poorly. That's why Ty and I are here," Becca said.

"I'm sorry for being so rude," Justin said, easing up a little after a moment's pause. "I don't trust people who keep secrets like that one."

Becca nodded. "I don't trust men."

Cam looked over at her. "Do you now?"

"Yes," she said.

"That's all that matters," Cam said. He pulled Becca back into his arms and danced her away from Justin.

After that, Cam held her close for the rest of the night until it was time to go home. He collected Ty from Jasmine, and when he left with his son and Becca, for the first time since his dad died, Cam felt like he had something of his own.

When they got home, he watched Becca tuck their son in and felt another surge of some emotion he refused to define. She turned to catch him staring at her.

"What?"

He waited until she was out of Ty's room, and then he pulled her into his arms and whispered hot needy words in her ear. Told her exactly what she made him feel and how happy he was that she'd come back into his life.

He carried her into her bedroom and placed her on the center of the bed. He reached up under her dress and pulled off her panties and then opened his own pants and slid inside her. He rested there for a minute and looked down at her.

He kissed her long and hard, the way he'd wanted to

since he'd pulled her into his arms. His tongue rubbed over hers as his hands swept over her body.

"Thank you for my son," he said.

"You're welcome," she said. "Now make love to me."

And he did. He made love to her, and then when they were done, he undressed them both and slowly built them to a fevered pitch again. He held her in his arms all night and didn't question the fact that he'd never had a relationship with a woman feel as right as the one he had with Becca.

He held her through the night, awake while she was sleeping, and watched her. She had changed his life, and he had no idea what he was going to do with her.

Marriage didn't seem to be the solution. Becca was used to being alone and he didn't want her to feel trapped. There was a reason beyond his callous behavior that she'd kept Ty to herself.

Though his brothers were getting married, he knew that the institution wasn't necessarily for him. He did know that he wanted Becca to stay in his life and in his home, and he wanted to figure out a way to make her presence here more permanent.

He drifted off to sleep without finding a solution, which later on would bother him. He was the kind of man who always had to solve a problem before he could sleep. But not with Becca.

It was odd to him, but he finally thought he was coming to trust her. And that scared him almost as much as the fact that he needed her.

* * *

Her cell phone rang a week later, and she glanced at the caller ID. It was Cam. "Hello."

"Hi, Becca. I have an emergency meeting with the community leaders at the Mercado. We are supposed to have one of the tenth-anniversary events there and I thought you might want to come and join me."

The week had been hectic. Nate's wedding was beautiful and had made Becca long for something more with Cam. She knew she should be content with what they had—it was more than she ever dreamed of. But a part of her—that little girl who'd waited for her own family to be complete, she suspected—wanted Cam as her husband.

She'd continued to work on designs for the Mercado and was slowly settling into a routine here in Miami. Cam had adjusted his schedule and had early dinners with her and Ty before he went to the club at night. He was making time for Ty, which was what she'd asked for, and she saw the signs that he could be a very good dad.

Though they hadn't really discussed it, she felt as if they'd found a new truce and were moving toward a committed relationship. There was a certain peace between them. Justin still didn't seem to trust her, but Nate and Jen had been friendly each time she'd seen the newlyweds.

"Okay. Why?" she asked.

"I want you to talk to the community leaders and get some of their input on the stores you will be designing."

"That sounds great. When should I come down there?" she asked. Work had been her solace and her guiding light, and she needed it to help her get back on task. She needed to focus and not let Cam throw her so off balance.

"Now would be perfect."

Of course it would be. "Um...I just gave Jasmine the afternoon off."

"That's okay. You can bring Ty with you."

"We will be right down there," she said.

"Good. I'm sorry about the last-minute notice."

"It's okay. Just let me get dressed—"

"Whoa, are you working naked?"

She laughed. "No. Why did you think that?"

"I'm a man," he said.

"And men think about sex all the time?" she asked.

"Exactly."

"So are you not thinking about it now that we've become lovers again?" she asked, kidding him. They had never had a teasing relationship before and she was interested to see another side of Cam.

"Hell, no. In fact, I'm thinking about you even more often than before. I can't for the life of me figure out why I let you go two years ago," he said.

"You were a fool," she said. She wished that he would have kept in touch or that she hadn't let her pride keep her from contacting him. Because the future—Cam's, Ty's and hers—would be a lot easier to navigate if she had.

"I was."

"I'm glad to hear you say that, but I was only kidding," she said.

"I wasn't. I don't know why I couldn't see you for the gem you are," he said.

Her heart melted a little bit. "I think it goes back to the guy thing where you just think about sex."

"Probably. Maybe fate stepped in to give us a second chance," he said.

"How do you figure?" she asked.

"It gave us Ty."

The more she got to know Cam, the more she really liked him. When the time came and she found the words to tell him that she had fallen for him again, she hoped he'd believe her and react like the man of her dreams.

Cam hung up the phone with Becca. He wanted to get something for her. But he'd already sent her flowers, and he really didn't have any other ideas.

He walked through the club and heard samba music playing in the rehearsal room. He paused and debated for a minute if he should interrupt Jen to talk to her. Finally he decided it was okay and opened the door. Jen danced around the rehearsal room. His new sister-in-law smiled at him as he entered the room.

"Are you here as my boss or brother-in-law?" she asked.

"Brother-in-law," he said. "I need some advice."

She hit a button and the music stopped. "What's up?"

"I need…what kind of gifts does a woman really like to get?"

"I think it depends on the woman," she said. "I like music and things related to dance. But I suspect that Becca might like something different. What does she like?"

Cam thought about it for a minute before he had his own idea. She liked art and drawing, and finding the right gift for her would be easy now that he knew what direction to go in.

"Thanks, Jen. That was exactly what I needed to know."

"I don't think I said anything worthwhile," she said.

"Yes, you did," Cam said. He hugged her and then turned to leave the rehearsal room.

"Why are you hugging my wife?" Nate said, coming into the room.

"Because she's brilliant." Cam walked over to Nate, who was scowling in the doorway.

"I know that. That's why I hug her," Nate said.

"I thought you hugged her for a different reason," Cam said.

"So did I," Jen said, laughing. "Did you come to help me learn my new dance?"

"No, I stopped by because I missed you. Why were you hugging my brother?"

"He needed some advice on a gift."

"What gift?"

"None of your business," Cam said. "Go hug your wife."

"I will. And I'm going to talk to her about letting just anyone hug her," Nate said.

"I'll leave you two to discuss that," Cam said, heading toward the door.

"Sounds good. I wanted some alone time with my wife," Nate said.

Cam walked out and couldn't help smiling. At this moment his brother was very happy. Nate's romantic past hadn't been so rosy. He'd been dumped by his fiancée when he'd been injured and had to leave pro baseball. And that had cemented in Cam's mind the fact that most women were only out for what they could get from their men.

Jen seemed different, and she made Nate happy, so Cam was hoping for the best. Was Becca cut from the same cloth? He thought so. She was sweet and sexy and seemed as honest as the day was long now that she'd opened up to him about Ty.

She'd changed over the past few weeks, or maybe he was just getting to know her. He had found that Becca was just the woman he needed. She was very good at creating a family bond. Each morning, they had breakfast by the pool and then every evening she cooked them an early dinner and they ate with Ty sitting at the table. She asked questions about his day and made a point to let Ty babble on in his baby talk so he had a chance to talk, as well. It was…something unexpected.

He wanted to find a gift for her that would let her know how important she was to him. When he thought of Becca and art, he thought of Chagall with his romantic abstract images. The perfect painting came to mind.

He called Val Martin, a friend of his from college who was now an art dealer. "How quickly can I get a framed lithograph of Chagall's *Les Trois Cierges?*"

"I might have one. Let me look through the catalog. Does it have to be that picture?"

"Yes," he said. He wanted Becca to have that picture. He wanted it hanging in her home.

The scene was colorful with a big green tree dominating the top of the painting. It had pretty white blooms on it and angels flew under its branches. A sleepy little town painted in a warm reddish brown could be seen in the distance. Three candles—from the title—were in the front left corner. But it was the couple on the right that had him convinced this was the right portrait for Becca. The man had dark hair and wore a brightly colored coat and held the woman tenderly in his arms. She wore a white flowing dress and her head was tucked on his shoulder.

"Do you want it framed?"

"Yes, that would be perfect. It's a gift, Val. So it's important that I get it as quickly as possible."

"I don't have one for sale in my shop but I do personally own a number of Chagall prints," Val said.

"I know. That's why I called you."

"I have a litho of *Les Trois Cierges* that is number 3 in the limited 450-print run, but it is one of my favorites."

"Would you be willing to sell it to me?" he asked. "I know that you have a ton of art work and can easily move another print or painting into its place. And who knows, maybe this will make room in your collection for another Chagall."

There was silence on the phone while Val thought it over. "Okay. I will sell it to you for $1,700. That's a bargain."

"Thank you, Val," he said. He would have paid double that to get the perfect gift for Becca. "How soon can I have it?"

"How soon do you need it?"

"I'd love to have it today," he said.

"If you want to come by my condo in Miami Beach, you can have it today."

"Thank you, Val. I'm on my way."

"Why is this so important to you, Cam? You've never been a big collector before."

He didn't want to share the details of his personal life with anyone, even an old college friend. "It's a gift for someone and I need it today."

"Someone? You mean a woman?" Val asked.

"Yes, a woman. And that's all I'm going to say on the matter. I will be at your place in forty minutes."

He pocketed his cell phone and went to deal with other details at the club. Little things that needed his attention—made him realize that this time he wanted every detail of his relationship with Becca to be perfect. He was realistic enough to know that they weren't going to have smooth sailing, but he wanted to make up for the way he'd let things end between them before.

The Chagall print would do that. In his mind he could see the image of the man holding the woman in his arms, and he hoped that Becca would never feel alone once she had it hanging on her wall. That Becca would know that he was always right there for her.

He left the club and got in his Tesla. He put the top down and drove out of Little Havana toward Miami Shores. He was a man who was very used to making things happen, and this was no different...Becca was no different. He was going to make her his completely. And if he made any missteps this time, he would make it up to her. It was important that Becca realize this time he was back in her life to stay.

He drove the hour or so to Val's house, handling business on his Bluetooth headset as he wove in and out of traffic. He arrived at her condo and parked, sitting outside for a few minutes while he finished up a call with Justin. Finally he got out of the car and went to Val's door. She had the painting all wrapped up and he handed her a check.

"Thank you," he said.

"You're welcome. I'm always happy to see a piece go to someone who will appreciate it."

He picked up the painting and put it in the trunk of his car. Val didn't ask too many questions, and Cam was glad. He wasn't ready to talk about Becca with anyone. What he felt for her was too private to be shared.

Ten

When Cam got back from picking up the picture, he walked the short distance between Luna Azul and the Mercado. Now that Justin and Selena had returned to Manhattan, he had to oversee more of the marketplace project than he had previously. But that sat well with him because he liked to keep busy.

He had to remind himself that just because Becca had come back into his life, he wasn't going to change the basics of who he was. Today had reinforced that. He had no idea if she was aware of how much she shook him up. But he was determined to control his reactions to her and to keep her in just one corner of his life.

He liked the fact that they were going to be able to work together, and he hoped her designs for the Mercado were acceptable to the shop owners. But he knew that, in his personal life, he had to ensure that she was...what?

Cam was interrupted in his thoughts by Selena's grandfather, lead shop owner in the Mercado project. "I'm glad you are here. The construction company is insisting on tearing down the sidewalk leading to my Cuban Grocery Store," Tomas Gonzalez said as he approached. "How are my customers going to get into the store if there is no sidewalk?"

He shook Tomas's hand. "We'll figure it out. Who is in charge?"

"Junior. And that boy never did have any sense. I'm tempted to call his father," Tomas said.

Cam bit back a laugh. Working on a project in a community where everyone knew everyone else, it was inevitable that emotions ran high. "I'll take care of it."

"Good. I knew you would do right by me," Tomas said. "We are family now."

"That's right, we are. Why don't you go back to the grocery store and I'll come and find you when I'm done talking to Junior."

Cam was given a hard hat by the work site foreman, and Junior Rodriquez met him halfway across the lot. "That old man is making me crazy. The sidewalk is cracked and a safety risk. I'm tempted to not let my men go in there to buy lunch."

"We need to figure out a solution that will fix the sidewalk and keep his store open to customers."

"He won't even talk about anything, Cam. He just wants his store left alone."

"That's why you and I are going to work this out. Can you do it tonight after the store closes?"

"It would mean overtime and I would go over budget," Junior said. "I pride myself on bringing jobs in on time and on budget."

Which was one of the things that Cam appreciated about Junior. He was a hard worker and he did the job right the first time. "Okay. I will pay your men in a separate contract to do the sidewalk tonight. You tell me the rates and we'll do it. Just the part in front of the store—the rest of it you can do tomorrow during the regular workday."

"Let me talk to my guys. I will get back to you in ten minutes or so," Junior said.

Cam left the other man and walked out of the construction area just as he saw Becca walking toward the shopping site, holding Ty on her hip. Seeing her with their son never failed to stir strong emotions in him.

He had already admitted to himself that he cared for her and he wasn't going to deny it now. There was something about Becca that made him want to be a better man. And he realized he wanted a relationship that was more real than his parents' had been. He didn't want to have his own independent life…he wanted to be a part of hers.

She and Ty both waved when she saw him. The boy made Cam smile with his sweetness. He'd never been aware of kids before Ty, but there was something about seeing his son that made him think of the future in a way that didn't involve shopping malls or night clubs. Not just plans for a bigger and more profitable

Luna Azul, but a personal future that didn't involve his club—a future that included something more than work. A future with Becca and Ty.

"Hello," he said, as they got closer. She wore a short pencil skirt that ended just below the knee, a big red belt and a button-down blouse. The belt drew his eyes to her tiny waist. Her hair was pulled back in a clip, and a layer of filmy bangs fell over her eyebrows. She had on a pair of large black sunglasses, which kept him from seeing her eyes.

"Hello. I didn't realize there was so much construction going on," she said. "I would have dressed a little differently."

"I'm glad you didn't. I like this outfit," he said.

"I thought you would but these heels are going to make navigating the parking lot pretty difficult."

He offered her his arm. She slipped her hand through the crook of his elbow, balancing Ty on her other hip.

"We have to tear down a lot of the older buildings because they aren't up to code. So I figured we'd get that out of the way while we were soliciting designers."

"That makes sense. Who did you want me to talk to?"

"Tomas," Cam said. "He owns the Cuban Grocery over there. Come on, I will introduce you."

He held her arm as they walked over the cracked sidewalk at the entrance of the grocery store.

"Some of these places are in a sad state of disrepair," Becca said.

"Yes, they are. But we got a good deal on the

marketplace, so we have the money to invest to make this a premier shopping venue."

"I can see that. What do you envision?"

"Did you have a chance to look at the portfolio?" he asked.

"Yes, I made some preliminary sketches based on a market I saw in Seville last year when I was in Spain."

Becca had always been a hard worker. Cam remembered that Russell said she was an asset to his team because she brought authenticity to the work she did. "Why did you stop working for Russell?"

She shrugged. "That's an odd question."

"No, I was thinking about how dedicated you are to your job and how starting your own business while starting a single-parent family was a double whammy. Why did you do it?"

She looked over at him. "I couldn't continue my busy schedule with Russell and be the kind of mom I wanted to be to Ty."

Cam tilted his head to study mother and child. She had said she was alone, but he realized as Ty continued to grow she'd always have her son by her side. He felt a pang knowing that they shared a bond he could never be a part of, but he knew he was building his own relationship with Ty.

"Russell would have let you work part-time."

She shook her head. "I couldn't do it. I didn't want him to know I was pregnant and put two and two together. And I had agreed to a certain work schedule with Russell and I know I wouldn't have been able to just do half the work I had done previously. It wouldn't have been fair."

"You wouldn't have been working to your own standards?"

"Yes. I would have ended up working all the time and never seeing Ty. And that didn't sit well with me. If I was going to have a child, I intended to be the best mother I could to him."

He hadn't thought he could respect her any more than he already did, but hearing her thoughts on working and parenting made him even more convinced of her basic integrity.

Becca was the embodiment of everything he'd ever imagined when he thought of the perfect woman. He leaned over to kiss her briefly on the lips.

"What was that for?"

"For being you," he said. He wasn't going to say more than that. Already Becca was making him reveal things about himself that he'd rather keep hidden. He would never have admitted even to himself that he felt safer working all the time. Until Becca and Ty had come into this life and his home, he hadn't realized what he'd been missing.

Becca put Ty down as she sat in the café area at the back of the Cuban Grocery store. Tomas sat across from her, and even Cam managed to get his tall frame into one of the tiny café-style chairs. The store was in disrepair and needed fixing up, but there was a warmth in the café that made her feel at home.

The Cuban grocery store didn't feel like any supermarket she'd shopped in during her life. It definitely made her want to come back here.

"What is your vision for this place, Tomas?" she asked. She'd found that once she talked to the people who were going to work in the clubs, hotels or buildings she designed, she had a better insight into what was needed from her.

"My vision?" he asked.

"Yes, tell me what you want your consumers to feel when they are here."

He rubbed his chin and then glanced around the store. "I guess I just want it to feel like home so that they can remember the old ways and not lose so much of who we are to American commercialism."

Becca was surprised to hear him say that so bluntly. "You know that Luna Azul also brings a lot of celebrities into the area. Is there a way that you can incorporate that consumer into your market?"

"I think that you and your brothers are looking to do something a little different here," Tomas said, looking at Cam. "But we also carry specialty food items that can't be found in other places, so I think that will appeal to some of the Luna Azul clientele," Tomas said.

"We are thinking about doing something different here. That's why I hope you will talk to Becca about the store you had in Cuba," Cam said.

"It wasn't my store but my papa's," Tomas said. For the next twenty minutes, Tomas talked about pre-revolution Cuba with a fondness that was infectious. Becca took notes as he spoke.

Ty was getting a little restless, which distracted her. She had to keep getting up to take things from him.

"I have to go check in with Junior outside. How about if I take Ty so you and Tomas can talk?" Cam suggested.

"Are you sure?" Becca asked. It would be a lot easier for her to take notes and concentrate on what Tomas was saying if she didn't have to worry about Ty doing something he shouldn't.

"Yes, I am," Cam said. He walked over to Ty. "Come on, buddy, let's go outside where you won't be getting scolded."

"Thank you, Cam."

"No problem," he said. She watched them walk away. Seeing Ty's little hand in Cam's, she felt a pang in her heart. She continued staring as Cam bent down and scooped Ty up when they reached the door leading outside.

"You and Cam have something between you," Tomas said.

"Business, but also our son," she said. She wasn't doing a good job of keeping her feelings for Cam hidden. She liked looking at him and being close to him.

"More than business, I think. Why do you try to hide your feelings?" Tomas asked.

She shrugged. She was used to being on her own, and a part of her was very afraid if she let Cam in and he left, then she'd feel even more lonely. "It's hard to own your own business and be involved with a potential client. I don't want to give the impression that Cam has brought me here for any reason other than my skills as a designer."

Tomas laughed. "You remind me of Selena, my granddaughter. She is the same way. Very much wants her business and personal lives to stay separate."

"Do they?" Becca asked. "I think I could use some advice from her."

Tomas shook his head. "Alas, they don't for her. At least not where Justin Stern was concerned. And I think it's the same way for you. No matter how many limits you put on Cam, he will always be more to you than a potential client."

"I agree. I just didn't want the world to know," she said, desperately trying to think of a way to turn the conversation back to business and not offend Tomas.

"What else do you want to know about Cuba?" he asked, changing the subject himself.

Tomas was at least seventy but wore his years well. He had thinning hair and a thick mustache, and he smiled easily, especially when he spoke of his family.

She thought about it for a minute. "Well, I want to know what your visual impressions were and why you remember those things. I think you mentioned you were a boy when you left. What is the one thing that lingers in your mind when you think of Cuba?"

Tomas leaned back in his chair and rubbed his chin. "I remember lots of flowers and old brick streets. There were some fountains and of course the shops had lots of outdoor seating. The open-air cafés where poets and revolutionaries sat around and argued about their worldviews. The coffee shops where my father would always buy me a cup of sweet coffee in the mornings and sometimes in the evenings as we'd walk back home from his store. I remember that the doors were always open and big paddle fans stirred the air."

When he spoke, she had an image in her head that matched a little of what she'd seen in Seville, and she knew what she was going to do. She started sketching as he talked, just a doodle really, but it captured what she needed for this moment.

"Will the redesigned store be more focused on groceries or the café?" she asked. That would make a huge difference in how the interior would be designed.

"The café," Tomas said. "When I was growing up I sat in the café part of my papa's store and listened to the old men tell stories while they sipped their coffee and smoked their big cigars. I want to ensure that the current generation and the future ones don't lose sight of where we came from. That the old stories stay important."

"Maybe you could have murals on the inside walls of the store, Tomas. Ones that captured the scenes you were just talking about. I think that would be a nice way to make your store feel different than the local chains. And to give parents and other visitors something to talk about."

"I love that idea. And I know the perfect local artist for the job," Tomas said. "Do you want me to give you his name?"

"That would be great," she said.

Becca knew exactly what he wanted. And she had a vision of how she could bring it all together. She liked working to bring the past and the future together. It was something she'd learned working for Russell. His Kiwi Klubs were successful because they took the best of the existing culture and melded it with the trendiest things happening in the world.

"Thank you for sharing your past with me, Tomas."

"You are very welcome. And good luck to you with your design. I hope that you create the one that captures everything the Mercado can be."

"Me, too," she admitted. She gathered up her papers and notes and walked out of the grocery store.

Cam was talking to a construction worker while holding Ty. They all had hard hats on, including Ty.

She blinked and then turned away, needing a moment to gather her emotions before she went over to them. Cam was exactly the kind of man she'd always hoped to find. He was sexy and dashing and charming. But more than that, he was a man who put family at the top of his priority list.

She'd had no idea he was that kind of man when they'd been involved two years ago. That was her own fault because she'd been embarrassed to be having an affair with one of Russell's friends. She'd tried to keep him a secret. So they hadn't really had a chance to know each other outside of the bedroom.

Her biggest regret was that she'd cheated both of them out of years they could have spent together with their son. And she could only hope that she hadn't cost them their future, as well.

Cam's cell phone rang as Becca came over to him. He handed Ty over to her and then glanced at the caller ID. "It's Nate, give me a minute."

She nodded, and he stepped aside to take the call. She seemed tired and a bit unsure as he walked away.

"Hey, Nate, what's up?"

"Not much. Jen and I are done early at the club and are having her nephew over for dinner. We wanted you and Becca and Ty to join us."

He glanced over at Becca. He wanted time alone with her yet he didn't. He needed time to figure out just how he was going to handle the intense emotional and physical rush he felt every time she was near him.

"Yeah, let me check with Becca and call you back."

"Yes. Definitely."

He hung up and walked over to Becca, who was making baby talk with Ty. They were so cute together. He stood there for a moment just watching the mother and child bond and feeling a little bit envious that his mother had never cuddled him close the way that Becca did with Ty.

"Is everything okay?" she asked when he approached her.

No, he thought. She had a way of finding empty pieces inside of him that he'd never been aware of.

"Yes, fine. Nate invited us over to dinner. What do you think?"

"I...I was hoping to talk to you alone tonight," she said.

"I want that, too," he said. "We will be alone when we get home. Nate will help you with your designs, too. You can get his insights into the Mercado, as well."

Becca looked up at him. She'd pushed her sunglasses

up on the top of her head, and he could see her pretty eyes. She was very serious. "I think I have enough insight. What's this really about?"

He rubbed the back of his neck. He hated not feeling sure of himself, and for some reason that was how she made him feel. "I want you to get to know my brothers better, and I want Ty to have a real relationship with his uncles."

She studied him for a long minute, and then she nodded. "Okay. Then I'd be happy to go to dinner at his house. I know how important family is to you," she said.

"You and Ty are important to me, too," he said. "I wish we hadn't lost so much time together."

He'd replayed their first relationship in his head a dozen times, and he didn't see any way for it to have gone differently. He had been a man driven to keep his eye on business back then. And she had been the same way. Just two workaholics scratching an itch, and he wished they would have been able to see into the future and this moment. Maybe things would be different now.

"You didn't want me to stay."

"I know," he said.

It was odd that they were having this conversation in the middle of a parking lot, yet somehow fitting. With Becca the most inconspicuous moments turned into the most monumental.

"You made me forget about everything except being together with you. That's not any way to live your life.

I would have lost myself, and I think that would have destroyed me and whatever we had between us."

Cam considered her for a long moment. He would have enjoyed having Becca lost in him. But she had a point that eventually it would have wrung them both out, and they would have broken up any way.

"You'll know when you're ready to meet someone who can be everything to you."

"Am I everything to you?" she asked. "Do you think I could be?"

"Yes, you are." And in that moment, Cam realized he was telling God's honest truth.

"I'm flattered," she said. "You are the first man that has made me feel this way, Cam."

"I'm glad to hear that," he said. He wanted to be the only man she thought of from this point forward.

She shook her head. "You confuse me sometimes. It's one thing to think of you as my lover but something else to think of you as Ty's father. The other night when we had that fever...you were really there for me, and I don't want to make that into something more than it was to you."

He reached over and hugged her with one arm. "It was nice for me. I don't think anyone other than my brothers has trusted me when they needed something. I mean outside of business."

She tipped her head back to look up at him. "I trust you."

"Let me call Nate back and then we can head over to his house."

"Okay," she said.

He stepped away to return the call but couldn't take his eyes off of Becca and Ty. No matter how unsettled he felt around her, he still wanted to spend all of his time with her.

"Hey, big bro," Nate said as he answered his phone.

"Hey, little bro," Cam said.

Nate laughed, and it was a good sound. Cam remembered how solemn Nate had been when he'd gotten injured and had been forced to give up baseball. Nate was a very different man today.

"So? Are you coming tonight?"

"Yes, what time?"

"An hour or thereabouts," Nate said.

"What can I bring?" Cam asked.

"Nothing. I got it covered. I'm a married man now," Nate said.

"Good. It's great to hear you so happy," Cam said.

"I think so, too. I can't believe how much I love my wife," Nate said.

Cam just chuckled. "That is good to know, but you should tell her."

"I will. In fact I have to go and find her and tell her right now."

Cam hung up the phone and walked back to Becca. "Is everything set?" she asked.

"Yes, it is. But I need ten more minutes on the site. I have to do some more negotiating with Tomas to get the sidewalk fixed in front of his grocery store, and he can be stubborn."

"Can he be?"

"Yes. Normally I make Justin do this kind of thing

but since he's still flying back and forth from New York..."

"You have to do it. Can I help? Tomas and I got along pretty well."

"Of course you did. You are a beautiful woman, something that Tomas can't resist," he said. Which was a good argument for using her to help get Tomas to agree to close one door of the store early. "Actually, if you don't mind just standing next to me and smiling at him I think it would help."

Becca laughed. "I'm arm candy?"

"Yes, you are, and very distracting arm candy, too," he said, bending down to kiss her. He didn't want to admit it to himself but having Becca by his side made him happier than he'd ever been in his life.

Eleven

Becca changed Ty into his cutest outfit and then sat on the bed. What the heck was she doing? She knew it was past time to tell Cam that she was tired of living in limbo and wanted to stay here with him forever.

Ty babbled his sweet baby talk at her and she looked down at him. The resemblance to Cam was striking.

"Hungee, mama."

"Hungry," she said, gently correcting him. She opened a package of baby carrots and handed him one to chew on. Then she finished getting his bag ready for their trip to Nate's house tonight.

When she was done, she smiled at Ty. "Are you ready to go?"

"Go," he said, nodding at her.

She slung his bag over her shoulder and then bent

over to pick him up. She'd dressed carefully for tonight, wearing a pretty sundress and leaving her hair to hang around her shoulders in soft waves. She'd applied her makeup with the precision and care of a runway model. She wanted to look good for Cam.

In the hallway she caught a glimpse of herself in the mirror. She looked the way she always did. Confident and average. Her son was cute as a button, though. In the mirror she didn't seem like the type of person that had always been alone and was afraid to spend the rest of her life that way. But did the mirror reflect her true self?

Cam had pulled the SUV up in the circular drive and waved when he saw them. He was on the phone, probably talking business. Was taking time out of his day for dinner with Nate going to mean he had to work later?

She hoped not. He'd promised her some time together alone. And she was going to insist that he keep that promise.

Yeah, right. That was never going to happen. She didn't have the kind of courage it would take to blurt out something like that. She'd told Cam she loved him before, and it had backfired...big time. She was going to just keep biding her time until she couldn't keep quiet any longer.

And it was torture. Because when Cam smiled at her, she hoped that he would always look at her that way. And realizing he might not hurt worse than anything she'd experienced since her mom died.

Once they'd strapped Ty into the car seat, Cam turned to her. "You okay?" he asked.

"Yes, why?"

"You looked sad just then," he said.

"I was just thinking about my mom."

He gave her a hug. "I'm sorry. Do you worry about leaving Ty alone?"

He had no idea how big a worry that was. "I...I really don't have any close friends."

"You have me," he said, gently stroking her cheek.

"We have to talk, Cam," she said.

"I know that we do, but that was Nate telling me not to be late."

"I guess family comes first," she said.

"Yes, it does," he replied.

"Oh."

"Becca?"

"Yes?"

"You and Ty are family, too." He closed Ty's door and rested his arms on the SUV, trapping her between his body and the vehicle.

He leaned in and kissed her firmly on the mouth, his chest rubbing over hers. She shivered with awareness as his mouth moved to her ear.

"I can't wait until we are alone later tonight," he said in his low, raspy voice.

"Me either," she admitted. He kissed her again before opening her door and helping her into the car.

She watched him walk around to the driver's side. The bond between them was growing much stronger, and she couldn't help but hope that this time Cam was going to be hers forever.

Being with Cam felt like home. It was a warm feeling, and she hadn't experienced anything this wonderful since she'd given birth to Ty.

Dinner was a lot of fun and kind of relaxing. They'd ended up playing Dance Dance Revolution. Which may not have been fair, considering that Jen was a professional dancer. But it had been a riot watching Nate, a former baseball player, trying to keep up with his wife and, surprisingly, with Cam. Jen shouldn't have been surprised that Cam knew how to move his body, but she was. She kept learning more about him, and sometimes it made her feel a little silly that she'd told him she loved him back before she'd had Ty when it was so clear now that she'd never known him.

Jen and Nate waved goodbye to Cam and Becca as they walked down the circle drive to their car. Ty was nestled on her shoulder, happily sleeping. He'd played hard with Riley, Jen's nephew, until Ty suddenly just sat down next to the couch and fell asleep.

She rubbed her hand over her little boy's sleeping head as Cam opened the back door for her to put him in his car seat. The last thing she wanted was to set him in the seat, but she knew safety came first.

She buckled him in and then turned to look at Cam. The resemblance between him and Nate was uncanny, but more than that the bond between the brothers was very strong. Family was such a huge part of who these men were.

And tonight had brought into sharp relief how selfish she'd been to keep Ty to herself for so long. But when Nate had held her little boy, she knew that he was happy to have Ty as his nephew, and that she would be forgiven.

A warm spring breeze stirred the air as Cam gave her a hug. "Thank you for a great night."

"It was pretty special for me, too. Riley was so good with Ty. I was worried about that."

"Me, too," Cam admitted. "I think I watched them like hawks for the first hour we were there before I finally relaxed."

"Cam, there is something I have to tell you."

"Good, because there is something I want to ask you. I hope we are on the same track," he said.

Becca wrapped her arms around his lean waist and rested her head over his heart for a really long minute. She wanted to stay right here in his arms for the rest of her life. Too bad that wasn't a possibility.

She inhaled deeply so that the masculine scent of him was imbedded in her senses and then stepped back. "I can't wait to hear what you have to say. I think that you and I are so much stronger this time."

"Me, too," he said. He closed Ty's door and opened hers. "We can talk more when we get home."

Home. She hadn't felt that way about anyplace but Garden City before, and now she was coming to realize that Ty and Cam were her home.

She sighed.

If everything worked out the way she secretly hoped, one day soon she'd be sharing major decisions with Cam about everything, not just Ty. And if it didn't—well, she'd continue moving along making choices. Some of them would be really good ones and others would be mistakes. And some of the mistakes, she thought, glancing back to make sure Ty was okay, would turn out to be the best choices she ever could have made.

"That was a big sigh," Cam said. "Are you worried because you didn't keep up with me during the game?"

"Not at all," she said. "I'm worried about where we are heading."

"Why?" he asked. "We're getting on well. Ty is adjusting. I think things are fine the way they are."

She shrugged, then realized he couldn't see her gesture, since he was driving. She had to respond but what would she say? "The more stuff we do together as a family...the more I wish we were a real one."

"We are a real one. You're Ty's mom and I'm his dad. Doesn't get more real than that," Cam said.

"That's not what I meant," she said. "I want us to be more than that. I think I told you I never knew my dad, but I created this image in my head of what would be the perfect family."

"What was it like?" he asked.

Like us, she thought, but didn't say that out loud. "It was a mom and dad who cared about each other and who loved me."

"I wanted that, too."

"Didn't you have it?" she asked.

"Not from my mom. She might have loved me, but I always felt that I was wanting in her eyes."

"I'm sorry, Cam."

"Don't be. Childhood isn't perfect for anyone. Haven't you found that out?"

She nodded. "But I want to do whatever I can to make sure that Ty's is."

He glanced over at her. "Me, too."

"I think you are a very good mother," he said, smiling over at her. He pulled into the garage at their home. He parked the car and got Ty out of the back. He was sleeping as usual, and Becca followed behind Cam as he took Ty inside and put him to bed.

She was glad he thought she was a good mom but realized she wanted him to think about her as a woman.

She went into the kitchen and took down two snifters from the shelf. She put in a couple of ice cubes and filled them with Baileys before heading back into the living room.

"I'm glad you got us drinks."

"No problem. I have something I want to talk to you about," she said.

"Okay. I wanted to speak to you, too."

She took a deep breath and a big sip of her drink. It burned because she'd swallowed too much, and she felt like an idiot when she started coughing.

Cam patted her on the back. "Are you okay?"

"Yes. I am okay. In fact, I'm better than okay. Cam, I…"

She put her glass down and then put her hand on his knee. "I love you and I want us to live together as man and wife."

* * *

Cam didn't know what to say. Love. Of course she'd have to say the one thing that he couldn't give her. She couldn't ask for diamonds or pearls or priceless works of art. She had to ask for something ephemeral.

"I'm flattered, Becca. I think this time you really do love me," he said.

"I do, too," she said. "I've known it for a while now."

"I'm so glad. I think we are making a very fine family with you and me and Ty. I was planning to ask you to make this move permanent and to live with me for the rest of our lives."

"I think it's a sign of how close we've become that we were on the same page," she said. Her smile was so bright that he almost didn't want to correct her. But he knew he wasn't going to marry her, and she needed to know that.

"Almost the same page, Becca. I'm not talking about marriage. It's not really for me. My dad was trapped in a loveless match with my mother, and I don't want to mess up what we have by making the same mistake as he did."

"What?"

"We both know you heard me. I'm not sure of us, Becca. Few people know this, but my parents married because my mom was pregnant with me. Having me and my brothers didn't make them any happier together. I don't want to repeat my dad's mistakes."

"I'm not sure what you want from me," she said.

"I want you to move into the master bedroom with me and I want us to raise Ty together."

She shook her head. "I don't think that will work for me."

"Why not?"

"I want more kids, Cam. I want Ty to have siblings. Plus your brothers are both married. I don't want to be the only live-in lover. I want to be your wife."

"I'm not going to get married to please you, Becca. I know myself well enough—"

"I don't think you do. I've never met a man more ready for marriage than you. You are just being stubborn because you are afraid to change your personal life."

"I am not."

"You are too. You are so foolish you can't even see that it's already been changed by me and Ty."

"I have already realized that. Why else do you think I offered…it doesn't matter," he said. "I take it your answer is no?"

She shook her head as tears started to roll down her face. "What was the question?"

"Live with me as we have been but move into my bedroom."

"How is this different from being your mistress?"

"We have a son," he said.

"Which is all the more reason I should be your wife, not your mistress. So I guess my answer *is* no."

"That's it, then. Nothing more to say."

He stood up and walked out of the house. She just watched him leave, knowing that she was out of words.

She couldn't talk him into loving her—not two years ago and certainly not now.

Becca watched Cam walk away and tried to keep from sobbing out loud. She tried to tell herself that it was for the best. That they would never have been able to work as a couple. But she couldn't help remembering the flowers he'd sent her. And the sweet way he'd taken Ty with him so she could work.

It was the warmth of her tears on her own cheeks that made her realize that she was crying. She hadn't meant to. She never thought she'd cry over Cam. She hadn't the first time they'd parted.

She wrapped both arms around her waist and sank down on the couch. It was amazing to her that she'd lost Cam in the same way she had before. She'd been searching for someone to be the missing link in her family. And she knew she'd found the right man in Cam. Was it because of Ty and the circumstances of his birth that Cam couldn't accept that they were meant to be together? She thought Cam had forgiven her for keeping the child a secret.

Perhaps it was something he'd never forgive. She tried to equate it with something that Cam had done to her, but could find nothing. Maybe he'd never really be able to forgive her.

She wished she could go back in time and let him know about Ty, but there was no use wishing for a chance to redo the past. That would never happen. She knew she had to move on. But she loved Cam. So walking away from him wasn't an option. Or was it?

She was always going to love him and she was going to be in his life as Ty's mom until she died.

If Cam had wanted to make her pay for keeping Ty a secret for eighteen months of his life, he couldn't have designed a better punishment than this. Having to see the man she loved and to know that she couldn't ever have him.

She got to her feet and went into Ty's bedroom. She stood over Ty's bed and remembered seeing Cam do the same thing when he'd realized that Ty was his son.

She tried to make excuses for Cam because she didn't want to spend the rest of her life without him. She hoped he was simply overwhelmed. She'd had nine months, give or take, to get used to the idea of being a mom. He'd had a couple weeks.

Even so, there was no doubt that he was already a great dad. It didn't matter that he was an executive and he had demands at work; Ty came first. She'd seen Cam keep his BlackBerry in his pocket for most of the evening and only checked it once during dinner.

But why couldn't he take the next step and be a great partner to her, too? She wanted to give them both the family they'd never had. To give Ty the parents she and Cam had lacked.

She couldn't believe it, but she still loved him. Even after he'd said hateful things to her, she really just wanted him back here with her. She wanted to feel his strong arms around her.

She was saddened that she wouldn't get to sleep next to him and wake up in the morning with him to Ty's soft calls. She wanted that for both of them, but it wasn't meant to be.

She leaned over the crib and kissed Ty on the top of his head and then retreated to her own bedroom, quietly undressing and changing into her nightgown. It was sleek and sexy, and she'd hoped to have a chance to wear it for Cam. It seemed now that would never happen.

She knew she had to stop thinking about him. And she needed to have a plan. She was going to have to be on her toes tomorrow.

She could stay. But that would make her feel like her soul was slowly dying if she had to spend day in and day out around the man she loved. The man who didn't love her back and was never going to.

She was so sad she started crying again and hugged the spare pillow to her chest as she fell onto the bed. She felt so alone and scared.

She had no one to ask advice from, and every decision she'd made...well, they didn't seem too smart at just this moment. And frankly, she was out of good ideas. She'd used her last one up when she'd decided to tell Cam she loved him.

She wanted to believe that tomorrow everything would be better, but she doubted that it would be. Cam wasn't going to suddenly fall in love with her. She was going to have to figure out a way to share custody with a man who was going to treat her like a stranger—worse than a stranger—every time they saw each other.

She rolled over, hugging the pillow to her stomach and stared at the clock. But no answers came to her. The last time she'd felt this lost and alone she'd called Cam. But she wasn't sure that he'd take her call.

Because it was midnight and because she felt like she had nothing else to lose, she picked up the phone and called him. He didn't answer. It went to his voice mail, and she hung up. She closed her eyes and wished her life were like the romantic tales she loved so much because then happiness and forgiveness would be waiting right around the corner for her and Cam. But she'd been alive long enough to know that dreams really didn't come true.

Twelve

He wanted to talk to both of his brothers, and though it was late, he knew they'd both be up if he called.

But he also knew that they had women in their lives now. And he didn't want to intrude. But this was big. He had a chance to change the course of his life. The way that Becca had changed her own life when Ty had been born.

A son that Becca had hidden from him. A love that she never did.

He called Nate as he pulled into his driveway.

"This better be a damned emergency," Nate said by way of greeting.

"I don't know what to do," Cam said.

"What? Where are you?"

"In your driveway," Cam said.

"Good, I'll be right down and we'll get Justin on the phone…is it Ty? Is he okay?"

"No, he's fine. I just don't know what to do about Becca," Cam said.

"Damn," Nate said. The front door opened, and Cam hung up his cell phone as he walked into the house. Nate hugged him close, and right away there was something comforting in having someone on his side.

"Okay, tell me everything from the beginning," Nate said.

"I will, but I want to call Justin, too. I'm going to need an attorney."

"This keeps getting better and better," Nate said, leading the way down the hall to his office.

Cam walked over to the wet bar and poured himself a scotch. He turned and held the bottle up toward Nate. "Yes, please. I'm going to tell Jen that I'll be a while. You can call Justin, okay?"

"Sure. Should I come back another time?" he asked.

"No, definitely not. I'll be less than a minute," Nate said.

He watched his brother run out of the room and poured himself two fingers of scotch, downing the drink, then quickly pouring himself another one. He poured a glass for Nate, too, and then walked over to the big walnut desk. He'd given the desk to Nate when he'd come back to Miami from playing baseball. Their father had given Cam one just like it when he'd graduated high school.

Cam hit the speaker button on the desk phone and dialed Justin's number.

The phone was picked up on the second ring. "Hello?"

Damn, it was Selena. "It's Cam. I'm sorry to call you so late. Can I speak to Justin?"

"Yes, just a minute," she said.

"What's the matter? Is Nate okay?" Justin said as soon as he came on the line.

Cam wondered if he shouldn't have waited until tomorrow to do this. But he'd known he needed to talk tonight, and this was a family matter.

Nate came back in the room wearing a dark navy robe. "Cam's got problems with Becca."

"What the hell?" Justin asked.

Nate sat down in one of the leather armchairs near the wall, and Cam stayed where he was, reclining against the desk. "Do you want the entire story?"

"No, I think I know what I need to know," Justin said, the bitterness in his voice coming loud and clear through the speaker. "The bottom line is, Ty is eighteen months old. What are you going to do? Are we suing for custody and taking the kid from her?"

Though part of Cam wanted to say yes, he knew he wouldn't be able to do that to Becca or Ty. And suddenly he had his own answer. He didn't need to be waking his brothers up in the middle of the night to try to figure out what to do next. He only doubted himself because he'd never had a good relationship except with these two and his dad.

"She's a good mom."

"I agree," Nate said. "But if you don't get along with her, you're going to have to take action."

The only action Cam wanted to take was to smash his fist through a wall. All because he couldn't admit to himself that he wanted to build a life with Becca. One that would include a cute little son named Ty. But now those dreams were dashed and he had to start over from scratch. Or did he? Because to be fair, he couldn't see a future with Ty without Becca.

Not without her.

"I don't know what to do. This is the first time in my adult life that I'm unsure what the next step is and I'm scared."

"Well, you're not alone and neither is Ty. We are going to figure it out and rally together. That's what the Stern brothers do best," Nate said.

Cam was grateful for his brothers, but he knew it wasn't going to be as easy to pick up the pieces as they made it seem.

"Do you think that Dad had it wrong when he said that Stern men weren't made for monogamy?" Cam asked.

"Yes," Nate said. "I was definitely made to be Jen's husband. I think Dad picked the wrong woman to tie his life to."

"Jus?" Cam asked.

"I agree with Nate. Dad was a great father but he didn't try to be the partner to Mom that I am to Selena. And that you are to Becca."

"How do you know?" Cam asked. "You didn't seem too fond of her."

"Selena pointed out that Becca was living with you and not angry at you at all. Do you know what kind of love she must have for you to do that?" Justin said.

"I do," Cam admitted. "I'm afraid to love her."

Nate started laughing.

"What?"

"You already love her. You just don't want her to know. You're not fooling anyone else."

"True that," Justin said. "You don't want to sue her, you want to live with her and Ty and are afraid to marry her. That tells me you don't need an attorney, you need to decide for yourself if you are going to keep hiding from life or grab it by the balls... My money's on you grabbing it."

"Mine, too," Nate said. "You have never been someone to stand on the sidelines."

His brothers had a point, and Cam knew he had already made up his mind. "Good night, boys. Sorry for the late night."

"It's all right. That's what family is for," Nate said.

"Just don't make a habit of this," Justin said, before hanging up.

Cam left Nate's house ten minutes later and drove back to his home.

In the corner of his bedroom propped against the wall was the Chagall print that he'd bought for Becca. Looking at it made his heart ache. He wanted to be that man in the picture holding on to the woman. And he wanted that woman to be Becca.

He took his cell phone out of his pocket and saw he'd missed a call from her but she hadn't left a message.

What would she say to the man who'd broken her heart? He loved that woman. It didn't matter what had happened and that she'd lied to him, he needed to have her in his life.

Becca was up before dawn and had all of her stuff packed. She knew she couldn't just take Ty and disappear so she'd made a call to Jasmine and asked to stay at her house for a few days. Jasmine had been surprised but said yes. She also knew she'd have to talk to an attorney and hammer out some kind of legal agreement with Cam. She was more than willing to do whatever she had to do so that Ty was the winner in this. He shouldn't have to suffer because love had dealt her a losing hand.

Becca had no other choice but to leave. She had figured out at about two this morning that if she was ever going to be able to function again, she was going to have to stay away from Cam. Being around him would mean staying in love with him, and that wasn't healthy.

She wished it had turned out differently.

It didn't matter what she wished. Real life had intruded on her fairy tale, and it was time to just stop pretending that it hadn't.

She opened the room to her room. Sitting in the middle of the hallway was a large framed print. She closed the door behind her and walked closer to it.

It was a Chagall. She didn't know the name of the painting, but she immediately knew who had given it to her. She went into Cam's bedroom to see if he was there, but he was nowhere to be found. She sat down in front of the painting. It was a print, she realized on closer inspection.

A man held a woman in his arms as they floated near a house. There were three candles in the foreground illuminating the scene. But what really caught her attention was the way the man held the woman.

He was protecting her and, to Becca's eyes, loving her. He seemed like a man who would do anything necessary to protect the woman he loved. And not just against physical dangers but also against loneliness.

She hugged Ty close to her chest and blinked to keep from crying. She loved Cam—and his giving her a gift like this sure wasn't going to make her stop loving him.

In fact, it made her want to do whatever he asked. Anything just so she'd have some small contact with him during the rest of her life.

She put Ty down when he started squirming. She stayed where she was, keeping her eyes on the painting.

"Hi, dadada," Ty said.

Becca glanced over her shoulder at Cam, who was approaching from down the hall. She had to fight not to cry. He looked ragged and tired. He wore an oxford broadcloth shirt untucked over a pair of faded jeans. And though this was the most casual she'd ever seen him, he looked perfect to her.

"Did you hear what he called me?" Cam asked as he picked up his son and held him.

"Yes, we have been practicing it." After a brief pause,

she said, "I...I love this painting. Thank you so much. But why did you give it to me?" she asked as he set Ty down.

Ty toddled over to them and tugged on Cam's pant leg. Cam ruffled Ty's hair, but that wasn't enough for the boy, who held his arms up.

Cam picked Ty up again and then kissed him on the top of his head. Becca knew it wasn't going to take these two very long to bond with each other. She was glad. Every child should have a solid relationship with his father. And she wanted that for Ty and for Cam.

"I had purchased the Chagall for you before we had our argument. And in my mind it was already yours."

"Oh. So it doesn't meant you've changed your mind?"

"No, Becca, I haven't changed my mind."

She nodded, a tear trickling down her left cheek. "I love you so much, Cam, it hurts. But I can't keep begging you to stay in my life."

"I don't want to hurt you, Becca. I want to be that hero who makes all your dreams come true. So I'm asking you to give me a second chance. Can you do that?"

"What? Oh, my God. Yes. Yes, I can," Becca said, a huge smile spreading on her face. "So you *have* changed your mind?"

"I haven't. It's what I wanted all along but was afraid to reach out and take. My only real desire was to be part of the family you and I have been building. I need to make you mine. To have Ty is a sweet bonus. So I'm asking you to give me a another chance. Let's start over this time with the air cleared between us. I think we have a real shot at happiness."

Becca ran to his side and threw her arms around his neck. "Me, too. You won't regret this."

"I know I won't," he said. "I want you to marry me, Becca."

"When?" she asked.

He laughed. "Is that a yes?"

"Yes, it is. I love you, Cam."

"I love you, too, Becca. I know our lives are going to be better than either of us imagined."

"Me, too," she said, hugging him and Ty close. Cam lifted her off her feet and spun them all around. Then he kissed her hard and deep, and she knew he was back to stay.

Epilogue

The Saturday morning of Memorial Day weekend dawned bright and sunny. Cam woke Becca early with a kiss.

"Why are you waking me up at 5:00 a.m.?"

"I have a surprise for you today."

"Okay. Do I have to get out of bed to get it?" she asked, sliding her hand down her fiancé's body and pulling him closer.

"Yes," he said with a laugh and a fierce kiss. "We can't be late, so hurry it up, woman."

She smiled at him and got out of bed. An hour later, they were all dressed and in the SUV heading toward Luna Azul. "What are we going to do at the club this early?"

"Something special," Cam said. He looked sexy in

his Luna Azul celebration golf shirt and a pair of faded jeans. She wore a matching aqua-blue shirt, as did Ty.

"I hope we can get a picture today of all of us. We look like a family," she said.

Cam reached over and took her hand and brought it to her lips. "We are a family."

He pulled into the parking lot, which was already bustling with activity, and led the way upstairs to the rooftop club. There the staff had set up a long buffet table with a highchair at one end.

"Good morning," Nate said, entering the rooftop club a few minutes behind them with his new wife. They both wore pink Luna Azul shirts and Jen had paired hers with a long ballet-type skirt.

"Morning," Cam said, and the brothers moved off to talk.

"Hi, Jen."

"Becca. I can't believe Nate made us get up this early. We were out until two with Hutch," Jen said.

"Neither of you looks the worse for it," Becca said.

"I'll need a nap later," Jen said. "Maybe I'll borrow Ty and lie down with him."

Becca laughed as Jen reached over and tickled Ty under the chin. She had never thought that she'd think of Jen and Selena as...sisters.

"I need coffee, Justin," Selena said as they entered the rooftop club. She wore a slim-fitting black skirt and a purple Luna Azul shirt.

"Yes, darling, anything else?" Justin asked.

"A kiss," she said, which he gave her before walking over to his brothers.

"Ladies. Can you believe the hour?" Selena asked.

"No. But I am excited about the weekend," Becca said.

"Me, too," Selena agreed. "I never thought I'd say this, but those three have made something special here."

"Yes, they have," Jen agreed. "I got a second chance from them."

Cam called them over to the table and they all took their seats. And Becca realized that Cam had given her so much more than a son as they sat there. He had given her that secret childhood dream she'd harbored of a family of her own. Not just a nuclear one of mother, father and child, but an extended one that would someday include cousins and aunts and uncles.

The staff poured mimosas for the adults. Ty happily held his sippy cup of juice in his pudgy little hands.

Cam stood up and everyone turned to face him. "I wanted to take a few minutes this morning to say thank you to all of you for your work on this celebration. I know that the hour is early but I wanted to start this celebration the way Nate, Justin and I started Luna Azul—just family.

"I'm so happy to be welcoming Jen, Selena and Becca into our ranks and to see the first seeds of the future of Luna Azul in Ty."

Becca smiled up at her fiancé and felt something close to true happiness and peace spread over her.

"To Luna Azul. May the next ten years be just as exciting and successful as the last," Cam said, lifting his glass.

"To Luna Azul," everyone said, raising their glasses and taking sips of their drinks.

Breakfast was a chatty affair and Becca enjoyed every second of it. Soon the festivities started and they were all pulled in different directions but Cam always stayed close by her and Ty. At almost midnight, Ty was sleeping in Becca's arms. Cam embraced them both, rocking them slowly back and forth to the music of the country music act performing at the Mercado stage.

"I love you, Becca," Cam said, leaning down to whisper in her ear.

"I love you, too," Becca said.

Becca had the feeling that she and Cam were going to be together long after Luna Azul celebrated its fiftieth anniversary, as would Jen and Nate and Selena and Justin.

* * * * *

COMING NEXT MONTH

Available May 10, 2011

HDCNM0411

With an evil force hell-bent on destruction,
two enemies must unite to find a truth that turns
all-too-personal when passions collide.

Enjoy a sneak peek in Jenna Kernan's next installment
in her original TRACKER *series,* GHOST STALKER,
available in May, only from Harlequin Nocturne.

"**W**ho are you?" he snarled.

Jessie lifted her chin. "Your better."

His smile was cold. "Such arrogance could only come from a Niyanoka."

She nodded. "Why are you here?"

"I don't know." He glanced about her room. "I asked the birds to take me to a healer."

"And they have done so. Is that *all* you asked?"

"No. To lead them away from my friends." His eyes fluttered and she saw them roll over white.

Jessie straightened, preparing to flee, but he roused himself and mastered the momentary weakness. His eyes snapped open, locking on her.

Her heart hammered as she inched back.

"Lead who away?" she whispered, suddenly afraid of the answer.

"The ghosts. Nagi sent them to attack me so I would bring them to her."

The wolf must be deranged because Nagi did not send ghosts to attack living creatures. He captured the evil ones after their death if they refused to walk the Way of Souls, forcing them to face judgment.

"Her? The healer you seek is also female?"

"Michaela. She's Niyanoka, like you. The last Seer of Souls and Nagi wants her dead."

Jessie fell back to her seat on the carpet as the possibility of this ricocheted in her brain. Could it be true?

"Why should I believe you?" But she knew why. His black aura, the part that said he had been touched by death. Only a ghost could do that. But it made no sense.

Why would Nagi hunt one of her people and why would a Skinwalker want to protect her? She had been trained from birth to hate the Skinwalkers, to consider them a threat.

His intent blue eyes pinned her. Jessie felt her mouth go dry as she considered the impossible. Could the trickster be speaking the truth? Great Mystery, what evil was this?

She stared in astonishment. There was only one way to find her answers. But she had never even met a Skinwalker before and so did not even know if they dreamed.

But if he dreamed, she would have her chance to learn the truth.

Look for GHOST STALKER by Jenna Kernan, available May only from Harlequin Nocturne, wherever books and ebooks are sold.

HNEXP0511

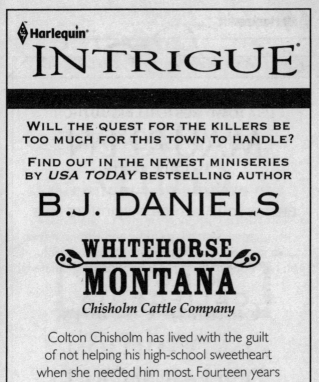